YAYO 2

**Lock Down Publications and Ca$h
Presents**
YAYO 2
A Novel by *S. Allen*

YAYO

Lock Down Publications
P.O. Box 870494
Mesquite, Tx 75187

Copyright 2020 S. Allen
YAYO 2

First Edition February 2020
Printed in the United States of America

Lock Down Publications
Like our page on Facebook: Lock Down Publications @
www.facebook.com/lockdownpublications.ldp
Cover design and layout by: **Dynasty Cover Me**
Book interior design by: **Shawn Walker**
Edited by: **Lashonda Johnson**

Stay Connected with Us!

Text **LOCKDOWN** to 22828 to stay up-to-date with new releases, sneak peaks, contests and more...

Thank you!

Submission Guideline.

Submit the first three chapters of your completed manuscript to ldpsubmissions@gmail.com, subject line: Your book's title. The manuscript must be in a .doc file and sent as an attachment. Document should be in Times New Roman, double spaced and in size 12 font. Also, provide your synopsis and full contact information. If sending multiple submissions, they must each be in a separate email.

Have a story but no way to send it electronically? You can still submit to LDP/Ca$h Presents. Send in the first three chapters, written or typed, of your completed manuscript to:

LDP: Submissions Dept
P.O. Box 870494
Mesquite, Tx 75187

DO NOT send original manuscript. Must be a duplicate.

Provide your synopsis and a cover letter containing your full contact information.

Thanks for considering LDP and Ca$h Presents.

S. Allen

CHAPTER 1

It had been a year since, YaYo had been indicted by the FEDs, still incarcerated at the M.C.C. Federal Building downtown Chicago, Yayo anticipated his trial date. Butterball had survived the attempt on his life in Cook County Jail and was due to testify at the trial. While being held in protective custody under heavy security, Butterball's only mission was being a stone cold gangster and he was ready to accept his fate of life or death.

It was 12:00 p.m and YaYo had just returned from his visit with his lawyer, Mr. Davidson. He'd told YaYo that the chance of him winning his trial was slim to none. He informed him that Butterball was going to testify that he was a soldier for the Get It Boy Click and that he was involved in the drug distribution and enforcement for the gang. Butterball would also testify that YaYo was the commander and chief for the organization and that he was the drug boss that orchestrated or participated in the murders of Jerome 'Jughead' Fields, Lotrell 'Homicide' Pope, Kenny 'Tank' Charleston and Jeffery 'Robin' Washington. If that wasn't enough, Butterball would also testify that the G.B.C was a criminal organization that followed a chain of command and disciplined members through physical violence and in some cases murder. YaYo was definitely FEDs bound and the thought of it all had him in his feelings.

As he walked back to his unit a lot of inmates stared at YaYo until he finally reached his cell. They knew he was returning back from an attorney visit and they were trying to read his facial expressions because that would exploit it, to the highest level of exploitation. YaYo was a master of the game and kept his face stone.

"What's good, Big homie?" Tey-Tey asked as YaYo entered the cell and plopped down on his bunk.

"Ain't nothing, this lil' faggot about to take the stand on a nigga."

"Yeah, That's fucked up bro. He gon' get his one day, YaYo." Tey-Tey had been YaYo's celly since he'd come to M.C.C. Tey-Tey was twenty-two years old and about to be shipped to the FEDs for a string of armed bank robberies. He wasn't a gang member and always stayed to himself, for that reason YaYo took a liking to Tey-Tey.

YaYo felt Tey-Tey had plenty of ambition and if focused on the right thing, Tey-Tey could become somebody great. Tey-Tey's introduction for fast money and guns kept him pulling down his ski-mask and running up in banks. If he was to get an immediate release, he would be running in a bank the same night. Unfortunately, Tey-Tey would have to wait thirty-six years before that opportunity would present itself again.

"Let me beat yo' ass real quick on the casino to get that shit off your mind." Tey-Tey offered grabbing the deck of cards from under his mattress.

YaYo and Tey-Tey played cards in the cell for an hour before YaYo got up and walked over to the payphone on the wall to call his wifey Shakira.

As Shakira was driving home from the grocery store and Shamira occupied the back seat, her iPhone sprung to life. After hearing *Kelly Rowland's Motivation* playing inside her purse, she grabbed it and answered knowing it was YaYo.

"Hello." After waiting for the automated operator to finish with the instructions, Shakira accepted the charges. "What's up, boo?" She asked with a huge smile plastered across her face.

"What did you say?" YaYo flirted.

"Nothing, baby, me and your daughter just came from the grocery store. Now I'm on my way home so I can clean that damn house," Shakira said as she jumped on the expressway heading South.

"That's what's up, I'm just calling to let you know how shit went with the lawyer?"

"How did it go, baby, what is he talking about?" Shakira said.

"Baby, he said it ain't looking too good. They got a dude in protective custody and he's gon' give it to them people on the real with my charges. Baby, they trying to give me a life sentence," YaYo informed turning Shakira's smile upside down.

"YaYo, your destiny is not up to no racist ass cracker baby, it's up to God. So, we put all our trials and tribulations in his hands. I just want you to know whatever the outcome I'm going to be there for you through thick and thin. I love you!"

YaYo let her love, devotion, and dedication smooth his emotions. "I love you, too, Shakira. I want the best for you and our daughter, and I don't want to be a burden on you with all of this jail shit. If you want to move on with your life then, baby, do that."

"Nigga, you got me all the way fucked up. How you gon' come at me with some crazy shit like that? That always been your damn problem. You always thinking about yourself. What about me and Shamira, huh? I don't care if they send you to the fucking moon, I'ma find a way to get there," Shakira cried into the phone.

"*You have one minute left*," the operator said.

"Listen, baby, stop stressing over the shit and just deal with it. I love you, Yaton. Everything is going to be alright—" The time ran out and the phone call was abruptly terminated.

Quavon walked down the hall of Kennedy King College on his way to lunch. His Rockstar jeans sagged over a brand-new pair of Air-Force 1's. The white T was the color of flake cocaine as YaYo's G.B. chain flooded in diamonds hung from his neck.

Meanwhile, Davon had transitioned well into college atmosphere. He was excelling in all of his classes. Unlike his twin brother who used college for the purposes of getting chicks and money. Quavon swag was dripping, so all the women wanted a piece of him. He graced the hallways of Kennedy King like he owned the joint.

Quavon made a lot of money in the school, he had been dealing with T.B. for the past year. T.B. had gotten his weight up in the streets and now sold work to most of the up and coming drug dealers throughout Chicago. Quavon met T.B. at his mom's house one day when T.B. was dropping off some money for YaYo, T.B. did that on a regular. Quavon begged T.B. to put him on with the work, after months of waiting Quavon finally broke T.B. down and got put on. Instead of the work, T.B. started hitting Quavon with quarter pounds of loud. Quavon would break the weed down into forty grams and take them to school. After a few months, Quavon's clientele was so official he graduated from grams to pounds.

Selling drugs was easy for Quavon because his smooth character sold the drugs for him. Everybody wanted to deal with Quavon, plus he had A-1 product. Quavon would pull up to school in his blue box Chevy that sat on 26-inch Forgiato rims. He was on a money-making mission.

T.B. watched as Quavon's bank grew making him feel like a proud father, so he flooded him with weight. Quavon also spent a lot of time with the G.B.C hitting the clubs and popping bottles with them on the weekends. They treated him like family, he was YaYo's blood, so he was also blood.

Quavon was at the lunch table glued to his iPhone, checking his Facebook page when Davon come and sat at the table.

"What's good, bro?" Davon said putting ketchup on his fries.

"Shit ready to leave, you got lab class today?" Quavon asked.

"Nope, but I'ma stay late today?" Davon replied taking a bite from his Pizza Burger. The two brothers continued to finish their lunch as three fine chicks walked up.

"Hey, Quavon, hey Davon," Missy greeted.

Missy was a thick redbone who was in Quavon's Business Management class. She was on a twenty-hour mission trying to get the dick from Quavon. Missy was one of those bougie chicks who always had her nose in the air like her shit didn't stink. For that reason, Quavon never paid her any attention. He was a player to the bone and his motto was never chose the hoes—let the hoes chase you.

"Sup, Missy?" Quavon said never taking his eyes off his Facebook page.

"Nothing just wanted to know if you wanted to go see that new Tyler Perry movie on Friday? My treat," Missy replied with sex dripping from her voice. Missy and her two friends took a seat at the table with the twins.

"Nah, shorty, I got a lot going on, right now. Don't got time for that shit," Quavon said smoothly, placing his phone on his Gucci belt.

"Boy, you always got something going on like you're just so damn important. You sure make time for these lil' busted ass bitches around here. You need to make time for a boss bitch like me," Missy spat, and gave her girl a high five.

"Bitch, my brother is about to go on trial for his life and you're talking about a punk ass movie! Get your goofy ass on. Matter of fact, move your goofy ass around!" Quavon said.

Missy was shocked at the way she was being spoken to. Her jaw dropped and her brows furrowed. "Fuck you, Quavon!" She got up from the table and stormed off with her friends in tow.

"Bro, you, silly as hell," Davon said cracking up at his twin brother.

"Man, fuck them hoes." Feeling his phone vibrate on his hip Quavon grabbed his phone, looked at the text and a wide grin spread across his lips.

"What you smiling about?" Davon asked being nosey.

"Man, I'm about to bounce. You gon' need a ride later?" Quavon asked grabbing his backpack off the back of the chair.

"Nah, I'm good bro. I'll catch up with you at the crib later."

The twins gave each other some dap, then Quavon rushed off to supply five pounds of Kush to his people. After conducting his business Quavon pulled up to T.B.'s condo on the Eastside. He had just made twenty-seven racks off the five pounds. Quavon also had a few G.B.C. members on 69th and Wolcott moving weed, so he was killing the weight as well as the breakdown. Quavon was trying to get a bag. He jumped out of his whip and knocked on T.B.'s door. A thick, chocolate sister answered the door wearing only boy shorts and a Victoria Secrets laced bra.

"Who you?" Quavon said as he slid pass leaving her with only the scent of his Burberry Cologne. The house was filled with weed smoke. T.B., Menace, Chopper and Reggie 'G' were all in the front room playing Xbox on a large television. "What's up with y'all?" Quavon grabbed the blunt of sour diesel from Maniac.

"What's up with you, Schoolboy Q?" T.B. joked.

"You, niggas gon' get enough of that, Schoolboy Q shit. Don't let the college shit fool you," Quavon said pulling on the blunt.

"Damn, pump your brakes *lil' soldier*, we know how you rocking," T.B. said emphasizing lil' soldier.

The five got high as kites and spoke about business. There was a lot going on in the streets. Everybody knew it was going to be a matter of time before the FEDs came kicking in doors with fresh indictments. YaYo's trial was in two days and the crew was mentally preparing themselves to support their leader. A lot of stress was on the G.B.C. as YaYo fought for his life. T.B. vowed that during the absence of their chief he would continue to push the line. YaYo and Quavon shared the same bloodline and if YaYo did get life, he would make sure his brother lived like a king in the belly of the beast.

An hour later, Quavon got up and gave his homie some dap. "Aye, fam' I'm about to get up outta here."

"Alright, hit my line when you ready for me lil' homie," T.B. said referring to the re-up.

"Alright bet." Quavon left out the front door.

After jumping in his whip, he pulled out of the driveway blasting his subwoofers never noticing the black Crown Vic with the occupants inside doing surveillance on the house he'd just left. Quavon had just got his first snapshot as a G.B.C gangster.

CHAPTER 2

YaYo had gone to trial and lost, so today he would face his fate. Butterball had punished YaYo in the courtroom. The nigga sang like *Patti Labelle* at a concert. Butterball told the FEDs that YaYo would go to Rockford, Illinois and cop bricks of heroin and cocaine and on the first of the month, they would take the drugs to a house on the Southside to weigh up and bag. He told the FEDs that YaYo killed Homicide a few years ago because Homicide tried to rob him. Butterball testified that YaYo murdered Tank because Tank had killed Joyce T.J.'s mother in a house in the wild hunnids part of the city, over money and drugs.

The whole infrastructure was broken down to the FEDs. Butterball told them about the lookouts, the security and the chain of command, as well as all the locations to the stash houses where money, guns, and drugs were held. He gave them all the pieces to the puzzle. He knew about Batman and Robin being on YaYo's payroll and how they attempted to extort YaYo for his money. That ended up with YaYo orchestrating the killing of the two crooked cops: Robin was shot to death and Batman clung to his life still in critical condition.

Butterball admitted he was on the mission with the deceased T.J. during Fat-Boy's murder which ended up being a double homicide. Butterball said T.J. forced him to partake in the killing. Thirty minutes had passed after Butterball's testimony. The jury came back with a guilty verdict. Now YaYo's future was in the hands of a white federal judge who sat high above him on the bench as if he was God.

YaYo remained in Boss Mode looking the part of a corporate C.E.O. dressed in a grey pinstripe Armani suit, Tom Ford squared shoes rocked his feet and his diamond Pinky Ring held enough ice to freeze Africa. He wore his hair in six large French braids braided to the back. YaYo took a sip from his bottled water and listened to the Federal District Attorney paint a picture to the judge.

"Your honor this individual is a murderous criminal to the highest extent. He has taken life after life leaving families to mourn for their loved ones. The man sitting here in the courtroom has no remorse for his victims and he has sold drugs that have poisoned our community. As the leader of the G.B.C. the violent organization whose objectives were to distribute drugs and murder rival gang members over drug turf. We must make an example that this type of lifestyle will never be accepted in our community." He glanced over at YaYo and saw him grin. "Your honor it is recommended by the United States of America that Mr. Anderson be confined to the Bureau of Prisons for the rest of his natural life. Thank you."

The judge shifted his eyes to YaYo's court-appointed lawyer. "Mr. Brown, would you like to say anything on behalf of the defendant?"

Mr. Brown stood up from his seat. "Your honor, what we have is a witness who was arrested and charged with a handgun and a couple of ounces of cocaine. Now this individual is on his way to a lengthy prison sentence and was less of a man to accept responsibility for his own actions." Mr. Brown spoke his words while eyeing, Butterball who sat next to his attorney twirling his thumbs and sweating. "He fabricated a story against the defendant to take the spotlight off himself. I'm not going to say, Mr. Anderson is an angel or that he hasn't had a troubled past, but he has already served his time for those crimes. Your Honor the testimony of the witness is not credible. He has admitted to being involved in murder and drug trafficking which are serious crimes. Mr. Anderson has a family that loves him, he is a good father and if pointed in the right direction could be a pillar of our community, thank you." Mr. Brown took a seat next to YaYo.

"Thank you, Mr. Brown. Mr. Anderson, is there anything you would like to say to the court before I impose sentencing today?" The judge said shifting his glasses on his long, crooked nose.

YaYo stood up, straightened the wrinkles in his Armani Slacks, looked at the judge and turned his back to him. "Yes, I would like to apologize to my family. Mama, I'm sorry for the decisions that I have made and I never want to cause you more stress and headache. I'm glad to be your son and I ask that you please don't give up on me." Yayo's loving and supportive mother, Karen's tears flowed like the Nile River. "Shakira you are my heartbeat, I'm sorry for putting you in this position and leaving you and my daughter out here alone." The thought of leaving his child and not being able to protect her from the coldhearted world caused a tear to swell in YaYo's eyes. YaYo wiped it away with the back of his hand and held his composure. "Quavon and Davon always know you can achieve whatever in life through discipline, dedication, and determination. I love y'all, niggas. Grandma, I love you. You made me a man and I'm thankful for the day you let me into your home. Please keep me in your prayers. I love all y'all and I will return home a better man."

Quavon put his head down in defeat. He had anticipated his brother coming home but he knew now that, YaYo would not be coming home. YaYo turned and faced the judge.

"Alright, Mr. Anderson thank you. You may have a seat." YaYo sat down. "Mr. Anderson I totally disagree with your attorney. You have been involved in violence since you were fifteen years old. You were released from prison only to start up a street gang that terrorized the City of Chicago. You have no remorse for your actions and I find that heartless. Mr. Anderson the United States Penitentiary were built for a man of your caliber. The world should be protected from people like you and it's my job to protect them. As for the indictment count one, continuing a criminal enterprise C.C.E, I sentence you to life in prison." Karen passed out. "As for count two, Tax Evasion I sentence you to life in prison. As for count three, I sentence you to three-hundred and sixty months— thirty years for possession of a firearm as a convicted felon. All sentences are to be served consecutively. Good Luck, Mr. Anderson." The judge slammed the gavel adjourning the court.

YaYo was led out of the courtroom with his head held high, leaving his family in tears. His total sentence was two life sentences plus thirty years.

S. Allen

CHAPTER 3

Batman was in the comfort of his home, he had retired from the Chicago Police department after the attempted murder on his life. He had just popped in a TV dinner and picked up the Chicago Tribune Newspaper from off the kitchen table. The headline read: G.B.C. Gang Leader Yaton Anderson sentenced to two life sentences for murder, drugs and weapon possession. Batman threw the paper on the couch when he heard the microwave beep meaning that his food was done. He used his crutches and walked over to the microwave. His nerves were still shook from the 7.62 rounds from the AK-47 that penetrated his thighs causing him to have to use crutches. As he was making his way to the microwave, his front door was knocked off the hinges. Moments later his living room was invaded with a swat team pointing MP-5 machine guns with infrared beams in his direction.

"Lloyd Thomas get on the ground now," the officer commended behind his black ski-mask.

Batman was dumbfounded as he laid on his stomach with his hands up. Swat moved through the home making sure no one else was on the premises.

"Mr. Thomas you are under arrest her extortion and tampering with evidence," the officer said holding out the indictment papers and search warrant. Batman was cuffed and transported to the M.C.C. building.

Butterball was standing at a bus stop on Cottage Grove, he was given immunity for his charges and was released from Cook County Jail a week ago. He had a new full-time job as a confidential interment...a fucking rat. He would be a snitch for the rest of his life, helping the Government take violent gangsters off the street. While Butterball was lighting a half Newport a black Tahoe pulled up, came to a screeching halt and three men jumped out wearing ski masks to conceal their identity. Butterball attempted to run for his life but three of the men snatched him up like a rag doll. Butterball was thrown in the backseat of the tinted SUV and the driver sped off.

When he woke up from his mini coma, Butterball was in the middle of a basement tied to a chair with five men surrounding him in the courtroom the guys surrounding him, he knew to be: T.B., Maniac, Choppa and Bootyman. The other one he didn't know but looked much like YaYo, then it hit him. He'd seen him in the courtroom.

The guy punched Butterball in the jaw, breaking it on impact. "Bitch Ass, Nigga," Quavon hissed.

Butterball tried to plea for the gang to let him live. His pleas for mercy fell on deaf ears and were exempt from the situation. Quavon tired of his begging walked up to T.B., snatched the .40 Caliber Glock from his waist and pointed it at the side of Butterball's head. *Boc*! The gun jerked in Quavon's hand as the hot shell casing fell to the floor along with Butterball's last thoughts and brain tissue. All the men looked at Quavon in shock at the sight of him catching his first body. The smell of death invaded the musty wet basement as Butterball's soul traveled to the afterlife. Quavon dropped the gun on the floor and wiped the lonely tear from his eye.

YaYo had just got off the phone setting up a visit with Shakira for next week when he ran into a cat named Fat-Pit. Fat-Pit was from 6 Mile in Detroit.

"Aye lil' nigga, plug me with a phone call."

YaYo had never even spoken to Fat-Pit so he found it odd for him to be pressing up on him about a phone call.

"Nigga, I ain't giving you no phone call. Nigga, I don't even know you," YaYo replied and kept going en route to his cell.

Fat-Pit didn't like his reply or attitude. "Fuck yo' lil' soft ass, don't get mad at me because your squad ain't hold up. Bitch ass—" was all Fat-Pit could get out before YaYo rushed him with blow after blow.

Fat-Pit hit the floor and got in a fetal position. YaYo preceded to stomp his face to the dayroom floor. Bloodstained YaYo's brown khaki pants while officers rushed the unit and forcefully restrained YaYo who was in a zone. Fat-Pit was left in the middle of the dayroom drooling in a puddle of his own blood until medical came in and placed him on a stretcher.

YAYO

When YaYo got to the Special Housing Unit known as the *SHU* he laid his blanket on a concrete slab that would serve as his mattress and laid on his back, staring at the ceiling thinking. "Damn, I'm on my way to the FEDs—fuck!" He screamed.

YaYo's knuckles were a lil' swollen and his heartbeat was racing from the work he had just put in on Fat-Pit. He closed his eyes to try and get some needed rest because he knew in the morning, he was on that bus going to Federal Prison.

"Yaton Anderson number 07505-424, time to go to prison boy."

YaYo opened his eyes and awoke from the boisterous voice of the fat U.S. Marshall who resembled Dan from the Rosanne Show. YaYo got up, grabbed his blanket off the concrete slab, and was led out of the small cell without the opportunity to brush his teeth or wash his face. He was taken to another cell with fifteen other inmates. They were loaded on a bus and headed for Terre-Hut airport in Indiana. While on the bus YaYo got to see Downtown Chicago for the last time, he would miss the streets. The same streets he and his squad dominated for the love of drug money. It took four hours to get to Terre Haute. When the bus pulled onto the airstrip the plane was already there. The U.S. Marshalls were posted everywhere with assault rifles and shotguns. If it was anybody with balls enough to try and escape their attempt would be futile.

'*Damn this shit real,*' YaYo thought to himself.

YaYo had heard stories about the FEDs his whole life but never would he had thought he would fall victim to their system and now he was shackled and being loaded into a plane with some United States most elite gangsters, robbers, and drug lords.

YaYo was told at M.C.C that he would be designated to a USP: United States Penitentiary. The name of the prison was Pollock, located in Pollock Louisiana and was said to be one of the most violent prisons in America. YaYo asked the guy sitting next to him on the plane where the plane was headed.

The man with the long dreadlocks said, "We are going to a hold-over in Oklahoma City till ya go to ya prison. What prison ya go to, Mi Boy?" The Jamaican asked his accent strong.

"I'm going to U.S.P. Pollock," YaYo responded.

"You go to a very bad place, Mi Boy. Be careful, a lot of killing in that prison, like a cloud of death over di place. Let God be with you."

The plane landed in Oklahoma City and for two weeks YaYo impatiently waited to go to U.S.P. Pollock. While on the bus he tried to mentally prepare himself to enter the concrete jungle of B.O.P.

CHAPTER 4

Three Years Later

It was 5:45 in the morning when the short, chubby Correctional Officer opened the cells in Unit C-1. YaYo jumped off his bunk, he was always up and ready when the doors popped. So much went on in the violent, deadly prison that you had to be on point, drama was first nature in the tense population. After taking a piss YaYo wiped off the toilet, flushed it, grabbed his washcloth from his locker and turned on the warm water. After taking care of his hygiene YaYo put on his tan khakis and laced up his prison-issued boots. YaYo was about to walk out of the cell until he felt his pocket, noticing something was missing. He went back over to his pillow and dug in it to retrieve the six-inch piece of steel that was sharpened to the point with a black lanyard wrapped around it. YaYo secured the weapon in a slit in front of his pants and dispersed from the cell.

YaYo had been condemned in the prison for going on three years. Since he had a life sentence he had to do no less than ten years in Maximum security before he was even considered being transferred to a lower level prison. The first couple of years in Pollock was a challenge for YaYo, He had to get used to being around other thugs and killas from different states. Being in a U.S.P was a different kind of battlefield. All the guns were checked in at the gate and replaced with jailhouse knives. YaYo soon found out that cats from D.C., Louisiana, Miami, Texas and other parts of the country moved way different than how he and his Chicago homies moved. YaYo rolled with the Chicago *car* which consists of all the dudes from Chicago. The GOS, BDs, Vice Lords, Stones, Latin Kings, and other organizations from Chicago. No matter what street wars were fought and how much blood was shed between the gangs on the streets, in the FEDs they all stood as one and united in arms in a coalition.

Pollock was a level 7 Penitentiary which held some of the B.O.P.'s most dangerous inmates, the prison was hell-bent as different gangs roamed the prison yard. The prison consisted of Crips,

Bloods, GDs and the Mexican Mafia just to name a few. Being that so many different gangs gathered in the yard the tension stayed high and for that reason, the prison was always on lockdown due to a stabbing or somebody getting bodied. YaYo walked down the stairs and went to check his email. After putting in his registration number he saw he had three emails: one from Shakira, one from his mother and another from his brother Quavon. YaYo read Shakira's email first.

Hey, boo I'm emailing to let you know I'll be working and I will be here until about, 9:00. So, call me then. We love you!

YaYo then read his mother's email. *Yaton, hey, son I was just checking on you. I haven't heard from you in a couple of days. Give me a call. Love you!*

YaYo then read Quavon's email. *What's good, big bro? Hit my line, I need to rap with you.*

After spending ten more minutes emailing his people back, YaYo walked over to where his homie, Pook was sitting in front of his cell.

"What's good, family?" YaYo said taking a seat next to Pook.

"Ain't shit. What's good with you, my nigga?" Pook was a BD from Chicago, he was from the Englewood area of the city 59th and Normal not far from YaYo's neighborhood. The two convicts had gotten cool with each other. Pook was a loose cannon, serving a fifty-year sentence for conspiracy in a string of gangland murders. He had a '*I don't give a fuck*' attitude and stayed on the bullshit.

Pook had heard a lot of stories about YaYo and the G.B.C. while behind the wall. One of the things that piqued his interest was that the G.B.C was also knocking off his enemies in the streets. The A.T.G.s so he had a lot of respect for the young boss.

"What you are doing on the workout today?" YaYo asked.

"Ain't no telling, probably go to the yard and do some navy seals and a few hunnid burpees." Pook was a workout fiend.

"That's what's up, I'ma probably do some pull-ups. What yard we got today anyway?"

"C-Yard," Pook said as Yayo watched his celly, Paco, come walking down the tier.

YAYO

Paco was from West Texas, and he was in the streets getting plenty of money until two rats landed him in a bogus conspiracy which led him to the Penitentiary with a fresh twenty-nine-year sentence. Paco took it on the chin like the boss he was and was confident that in the near future, he would get back in court and give the Government back the bogus time.

YaYo respected Paco and liked how he moved so the two of them were cooler than ice in a cooler.

"Pook, you going to breakfast?" YaYo asked standing up straightening out his Khaki shirt.

"Nah, I'm about to hop on this phone and call, baby girl."

"Nigga stop panty checking, too early for that shit," YaYo joked.

"Chow!" The Correctional Officer yelled as he walked out of the officer's station to open the front door and release the inmates for the chow hall.

Pook walked over to one of the four phones and YaYo went out the front door. Once YaYo walked out of the building he was met by the humidity of the Louisiana weather. It was only six in the morning and it already felt like it was 100-degrees. On the way to the chow hall, YaYo caught up with Hitman a cat he sold cigarettes to, from D.C.

"Aye Hitman let me holla at you real quick?"

Hitman looked back, saw YaYo and made a U-Turn towards him. "YaYo, what's up slim?" Hitman greeted shaking YaYo's hand.

"Ain't shit. What's the bizness on that demonstration I gave you?" YaYo asked pertaining to the three caps of tobacco he had fronted him about a week ago.

"Man, I got fifteen books for you, right now. I'm waiting to get the other fifteen later and when I do, I'ma straighten that," Hitman said and went in his pants pocket to retrieve the knot of stamps giving them to YaYo. Hitman was a good consistent business so YaYo wasn't pressing him about the other fifteen books. He knew he was good for it.

"A'ight, champ." YaYo grabbed his tray which consisted of a glazed honey bun, oatmeal, and a half of orange. After getting a cup of milk YaYo proceeded to the table where his homies sat. The chow hall was segregated, people from Florida, Alabama, Louisiana and D.C all had their own table as well as the Crips, Bloods, Mexican and Aryon Brotherhood.

"What's going on with you, YaYo?" Sinica asked peeling his orange. Sinica was a GD from the wild-wild hunnids.

"Chasing the money trying to stay out of the way," YaYo replied putting a spoon full of oatmeal in his mouth.

"Aye check it out fam, the word on the compound is that the Florida niggas got something going on, so be on point. I'm not sure but we might be going on lockdown," Sinica informed, letting him know something was about to pop off.

"Shit always popping off around this bitch. Niggas can't even get no money we probably gon' be lockdown and I still got sixty books in the streets. That's two-hundred dollars a nigga needs that." YaYo was agitated.

YaYo and Sinica finished their breakfast, got up, dumped their trays and headed back to the unit. On the way back YaYo noticed a group of inmates politicking on the side of the fence. He immediately noticed all the men were from Florida.

"You see that shit?" YaYo mumbled nodding his head toward the group as he and Sinica stood in front of C-Building.

"I told you, bruh. They been politicking since yesterday, they say that nigga, Bo from Miami supposed to be hot. So I guess we'll see what's up."

"Well, it is what it is. That shit ain't got nothing to do with the guys. So, I'ma slide up in the building before these niggas get to tapping. I'm going to the yard when they call the move. We got C-Yard."

"A'ight bet, I'm holla at you in a minute." Sinica gave YaYo some dap and went up to unit C-3 as YoYo went to C-1.

Once inside the unit, YaYo was approached by an older cat named Cadillac. "YaYo, what's up youngster you still good on them squares?"

"You already know old school, come on up to my cell. I got you."

Cadillac followed YaYo up the tier to his cell. Once in his cell, YaYo pulled out a plastic baggie containing rolled up cigarettes and gave Cadillac one. Cadillac gave YaYo a book of stamps and left the cell. After making the serve YaYo pulled all the stamps out of his pocket and put them on his desk. He was about to attempt to count them until he heard inmates beating on their windows meaning the deuces were going off. When he looked out of his window he saw Correctional Officers and Medical staff rushing across the yard. The same Florida cats that were on the side of the fence politicking where engaged in a full-fledged knife fight on the yard. At the sight of the officers running their way with riot pumps and pepper spray most of the inmates involved backed off to try and ditch their weapons and comply with officers.

"Lockdown, lockdown!" the officer inside YaYo's unit yelled.

YaYo continued to look out the window as an inmate was placed on a stretcher with his chest and face covered in blood.

"Damn," YaYo said out loud.

He grabbed his ice cooler and proceeded to the ice machine and computer to send his family an email informing them he was on lockdown. Just another day in Pollock.

S. Allen

CHAPTER 5

"Come here, Shamira, come to Uncle Quavon," Quavon said as he chased his niece Shamira through the house.

Shmira giggling the whole time. Quavon was at his mother's house for dinner and the whole family was present: Shakira, Shamira, Davon, and their grandma Honey. Karen stood over a hot pot of spaghetti. She had told everybody to come over for dinner and spend some quality time with the family.

Everybody was doing well. Davon and Quavon were in their third year of college. Davon excelled in his studies while his twin brother's grades were slipping but nevertheless, he stayed with it because he promised his mother and grandma that he would graduate. Quavon's main focus was selling work. He had graduated from selling pounds of weed to selling cocaine and Heroin. The riches he obtained from the hard drugs were far more than he received from the weed. T.B. didn't like the idea of letting Quavon enter the dope game but the streets were calling Quavon's name and Quavon answered the night he put Butterball's brains on the wall. At that point he knew there was no turning back for young Quavon, so he put him all the way in the game.

Karen knew what her son was involved in, he was living his life as his oldest brother and it hurt her heart because she knew it was only two outcomes of such a lifestyle: jail or death. He hid nothing from her. The only thing she felt she could do was hit her knees at night and pray that God has mercy on her son's soul. Karen loved her sons right or wrong and would always be there for them, but she let Quavon know that she didn't and would never condone the way he was living. She just hoped and prayed Davon wouldn't convert to the wicked streets as his brothers had.

Shakira would also preach to Quavon. Shakira was doing well working at *Style & Grace* with Karen. She liked doing hair and was good at it, so she got a lot of good tips from her regulars. When YaYo got knocked by the FEDs they took everything, the house, cars, and money so she had to start from scratch but with family support, it wasn't hard at all. T.B. YaYo's comrade also blessed her game by making sure she wanted for nothing. Shakira had gone to see YaYo twice in the last three years of his incarceration. The last time she flew to Louisiana to see him when she finally made it to the prison, she was informed that the prison was on lockdown. YaYo could get moved closer to family until then she would just continue to play her position as wifey and keep supporting her man.

Quavon went over, picked up Shamira and placed kisses all over her face which caused her to laugh uncontrollably.

"Boy, put her down," Shakira said with a smile on her face as she continued to get on her laptop to surf the internet.

"Y'all come to the table so y'all can eat!" Karen yelled from the kitchen while she loaded their plates with spaghetti and garlic bread. After making their plates she passed them out to her family.

Quavon picked up his fork and dove in until Karen popped him upside the head with a spoon.

"Boy, you know we say grace in this house before we eat."

"My fault ma," was Quavon's only reply while he rubbed the side of his head.

Shakira put Shamira in her highchair and took a seat at the table. After everyone was seated, Honey began to say grace.

"God almighty we would like to thank you for all this wonderful food you have blessed us with. Thank you for keeping us safe and healthy. Thank you for the love in our family. You are the creator of all things and we thank you for all your blessings. Amen!"

Everybody said Amen, then Quavon picked up where he left off.

"It's about time," Quavon said sarcastically putting a fork full of spaghetti in his mouth.

"What's wrong, baby?" Karen asked noticing the sad look on Shakira's face.

"That was, Yaton. He says they're going on lockdown again."

Everybody got quiet and was lost in their own thoughts. They feared for YaYo's safety while he was in Pollock. Quavon had Googled Pollock and found out it was ranked number 25 as being one of the worst prisons in the county.

"YaYo will be alright, y'all. He can take care of himself in there," Quavon said trying to keep his family strong.

Quavon knew the other side of his brother. He was a gangster, the goon. It was YaYo who instilled in him that the morals and principles were no different from the streets. Quavon looked at his diamond-studded *Movado* and saw that it was getting late. He had to make a trip to the Westside to check on one of his blocks and collect some cash from some of his workers.

After putting his plate in the sink, Quavon kissed his mother on the cheek and grabbed his *Pelle Pelle* leather jacket.

"Boy, where you think you going?" Karen said over her shoulder.

"I gotta make a run real quick, ma. I'll call you later." was all Quavon said before he left out the door to go run the streets.

S. Allen

CHAPTER 6

Top Cat sat in a basement on the Westside of the city counting the money that his lieutenant had given him from the workers that day. Shorty, Gang Bang, Muncho, and Dave were his trusted lieutenants who oversaw his Heroin operation.

Muncho controlled the area on Chicago Avenue and Springfield. Shorty and Gang Bang oversaw Homan and Ohio. Dave oversaw Averas and Thomas. Each one of Top Cat's lieutenants had a 50,000 a day quota that had to be met.

Top Cat stood up from the pile of money and the money counting machine. "Muncho, I seem to have a lil' problem, lil' brother."

"What's that, chief?" Muncho replied.

"The problem, motherfucka is it's Friday and since Monday you been coming up short. So, I asked myself is the nigga slipping up? Is his math fucked up? Or is he trying to get over on the program?" Top Cat eyed Muncho down with evil intent.

Top Cat had a zero tolerance for niggas turning in short money. At fifty-two years old he was a veteran dope dealer and with a trail of bodies left from him and his team he was also a feared man.

Muncho was nervous and chose his next words carefully. "Top, it's a spot-on, Troy Street that just opened up. They say the dime bags look like fifties and a couple of fiends have overdosed off the shit. So, all the fiends shopping on Troy Street."

"Whose block is it?" Top Cat walked up on Muncho.

"I don't know Top—" was Muncho's only reply before Top Cat produced a razor from his jacket pocket and ran it across Muncho's throat in one swift motion.

Muncho felt nothing as blood spurted from his throat. In a state of shock, Muncho gripped his own throat in an attempt to stop the blood from spraying from his neck. His attempt was frivolous as he fell to his knees and his soul slowly left his body.

Top Cat wiped the bloody razor on Dave's quarter link mink coat, calmly sat back on the couch and lit a black and mild cigar. "Now you two motherfuckers find out who's running that shit on Troy Street and shut that shit down, asap! Do you hear me? Shut it down, that shit fucking up my money." The two henchmen nodded in understanding. "And clean this shit up," Top Cat said referring to Muncho's dead corpse.

The gangsters did as they were told and went to dump Muncho's body somewhere in the murder infested streets of Chicago.

****

"What time is it, Paco?" YaYo asked as he finished his last sets of push-ups. It had been two weeks and the prison was still on lockdown.

"I'll be glad when they let us up. The lockdown shit ain't hittin' on nothing."

YaYo took a seat on his bunk, then pulled some weed from his stash and proceeded to roll a joint.

"Fam, this prison shit crazy. It's like these niggas ain't got nothing to live for. Dudes is getting crushed around here. Them Florida cats wasn't faking at all," YaYo said putting the final touch on his joint.

"Yeah, but all these lockdowns back to back got it to where niggas can't make no money or shit," Paco replied.

"You can look at lockdowns a few ways, my nigga. I feel you on not making no money but look at this way, every day we on lockdown is a day you, haven't stabbed one of these niggas. Or a day one of these ignorant niggas haven't stabbed you. Plus, a nigga can get some much-needed rest," YaYo replied before using two batteries and a razor to light the joint. Taking two strong pulls from the joint he passed it to Paco.

"Square blzness, my nlgga. You definitely on point about that," Paco said grabbing the joint from YaYo.

After getting high the two begin to play cards when the Correctional Officers slid a piece of mail under the door. YaYo got up and grabbed the mail off the floor. The letter was from Shakira. YaYo sat on his bunk and started reading the letter, the smell of Shakira's *Mariah Carey* perfume stained the pages invading the small cell with her scent which only made YaYo miss her more. Shakira told him about what was going on at home with the family and how much she missed him. YaYo continued to read the letter, Shakira told him to make sure he wrote his brothers, mainly Quavon.

She mentioned in the letter that Quavon was spending a lot of time in the streets and may need his guidance. YaYo folded the letter up and stuck it under his mattress. YaYo knew the extent of what Quavon was involved in. He knew his lil' brother was trying to fill his shoes in the streets. Knowing how his brother moved in the streets he knew Quavon was getting his weight up out there. He was the one that groomed him. The lucrative dope-game in Chicago was one that would ring bells for years to come with Quavon itching to be crowned king. After pulling out a pen and a notepad YaYo starting writing his younger brother to give him some words of wisdom.

****

Quavon checked his rearview mirror as he slid his black Charger through the grimy streets of the Westside. He was on his way to one of his most lucrative blocks. The one on Troy Street. It was late and Quavon closed all his spots at 9:00 on the dot and it was 8:30. Normally Quavon would send one of his lieutenants to pick up the money from the workers but tonight he wanted to be hands-on. So, he figured he would circle around and oversee his block. A Glock 9mm rested on his lap. Quavon made a left on Troy Street when he noticed two men in a beat-up box Chevy in his rearview.

Quavon watched them through the mirror and noticed the two men seemed to be in a heated argument when all of a sudden one of the men pulled a ski-mask over his head and his potna followed suit. Something definitely wasn't right, grabbing his cell phone Quavon placed a call.

"Nigga, listen, the chief said shoot everybody standing on the corner and that's what the fuck we gon' do. You gotta problem with that then take it up with the boss," Shorty, sneered behind the wheel of the Chevy as he and Dave were on a murder mission to shut down the spot on Troy Street. The two killas had a difference on how the hit was going to transpire. Dave wanted to rob the stash house on the block for the money and drugs then shoot everybody in the house. Shorty, on the other hand, wasn't trying to hear that shit. He had been taken his orders from Top Cat and those orders were to be followed, period.

"I'm just trying to say we can hit a lick in the process, get the shit from them niggas and put it on our blocks," Davo said pulling a ski mask over his face.

"Nigga shut the fuck up and get ready. You better empty that Tec, too," Shorty retorted pulling his ski-mask down.

The two argued like cats and dogs but when the work got put in, they crushed their targets. Most of the men on the other side of their weapons were closed caskets.

"Aye, you see them dudes on the corner?" Dave pointed to the eight men standing on the corner of Troy Street selling Heroin to fiends.

"Yeah, I see 'em." Shorty parked the car behind a blue Ford Taurus and killed the lights. He put the thirty round extended magazines into his Sig Sauer, Shorty chambered a round into the chamber.

"Man let's get this shit over with, I got a lil' redbone I'm trying to nail tonight," Dave said and got out of the car.

Shorty did the same as the two concealed their weapons and started creeping towards the corner to lay their murder game down.

"Aye fam check it out it's two niggas in a rusted box Chevy on the way through the block. The niggas got on masks. When they come through air that shit out," Quavon commanded to his security personal.

The security ended the phone call and grabbed his walkie talkie. "Two niggas in a rusty box Chevy shoot on sight." The security sent the message to the two snipers on top of the courtyard building in the middle of the block.

Quavon pulled in no less than fifty racks a day so his security was impeccable. YaYo always told Quavon to secure what he loved, and he loved money, so he kept shooters on deck.

"Say no more," the sniper said through the walkie talkie and pulled the slide back on the 308 Winchester and took position.

Quavon doubled back around the block, located the Chevy and parked two cars behind it. Turning the ignition off Quavon laid the seat back, pulled his hoodie over his head and watched the drama unfold.

After the two gangsters exited the whip the dark night was lit up with gunfire.

Cha! Cha! Cha! Cha!

"Ahhhhhh!" Dave yelled as the 308 slug ripped through his thigh.

The sound of the rifle sounded like thunder. The men on the corner all pulled firearms and let them blow on Shorty and Dave.

"Die, niggas—die!"

Boc! Boc! Boc! Boc! Boc! Shorty saw Dave's head split like a cantaloupe.

The sniper had Dave's head in the crosshairs of his scope before he pulled the trigger and splattered Dave's brain on the streets. Seeing that he didn't have a chance completing the death mission Shorty let the Sig spit venom before he got up and took off running toward the Chevy. Still breathing Shorty was able to open the driver's side door. Suddenly Quavon walked up, with his hoodie over his head and Glock is hand. He shot Shorty point-blank range in the head sending him into complete darkness.

Hearing sirens getting closer and closer, Quavon jogged back to his whip, put the murder weapon in his stash spot and calmly pulled off, passing the carnage that was left on his block as a feeling of power came over him. Two henchmen had just brung drama to his block and in return got jacked for their souls.

YaYo had told Queven years ago. "*If you obtain a lot of money in the streets niggas will forever test your gangsta. So, murder is always used as a tool for peace. The money brings homicide.*"

Quavon got on the Dan Ryan expressway thinking about his brother and how everything YaYo told him was always on point. YaYo also told Quavon that no matter what endeavors he chose in life to always master your craft. On the strength of YaYo, Quavon had vowed to be King of the Chi because had it not been for a rat putting YaYo in prison for life, YaYo would've sat on the throne. So, Quavon was going to make sure YaYo's hard work never went in vain.

CHAPTER 7

It had been a week since the institution was back up and running. YaYo was standing in the Commissary line. After a long lockdown, every inmate in the prison was sure to go to commissary to stock up on food and hygiene items. YaYo hated going to commissary because it was always at least fifty people stuck in one room for an hour and a half waiting to get their items

"What number you got, Sinica?"

"I'm number thirty-eight. I wish they would hurry up, it's hot as hell up here."

"Yeah, I know that's why I hate coming up here," YaYo replied.

YaYo and Sinica sat in the commissary kicking the shit waiting to get their items when YaYo spotted Curt with a laundry bag full of commissary.

"Aye Curt, what's good, Joe?" YaYo sneered walking towards Curt.

"What's up, YaYo?" Kansas Curt nervously spoke from his large crusty lips. Kansas Curt had been doing business with YaYo on the tobacco side and owed YaYo twenty books of stamps and had been ducking him for three months.

YaYo slid up on Kansas Curt with Sinica in tow with a menacing facial expression. "What the fuck you mean what's up, YaYo. You been ducking me for three months nigga. Now I find you in commissary with a bag full of shit, like you don't owe me."

Curt had been dragging YaYo and YaYo was vexed. "Man, listen I told you I got you when I get right. What I'm doing in commissary ain't got nothing to do with you, fam," Curt expressed trying to stand his ground in front of the other inmates who had got a whiff of what was going on.

YaYo put his hands up in a surrendering motion. "You know what, my nigga you go that. Go ahead and keep them books, it's all good player," YaYo said and walked off from the confrontation.

"YaYo, I know you not gon' let that clown get that shit off so you can step with the bullshit," Sinica joked.

"Man would you knock it the fuck off. When they let us outta commissary on my daughter I'm a knock his pussy ass out and if homies want some rec, they can get it too. You got your knife on you?" YaYo asked Sinica reaching inside the front of his khakis putting his hand on his weapon.

"Nigga you better believe it," Sinica retorted smiling from ear to ear.

Sinica had been in prison for two decades and had put in work in every U.S.P. he landed at. Sinica had a thirst for blood and violence and his knife play was always up his alley.

About thirty minutes later C.O. Clove opened the door to let the inmates out of the commissary to return to their units. The inmates grabbed their commissary bags and began to exit the room when YaYo walked up behind Kansas Curt and tapped him on his shoulder. When Kansas Curt turned to see who tapped him on the shoulder, YaYo threw a right hook that landed on the button on Kansas Curts chin, he hit the floor with a loud thud along with his big bag of commissary, unconscious.

The other inmates watched as YaYo picked up Kansas Curt's bag, stepped over his body and left the commissary with Sinica tagging along. The two convicts boldly walked back to C-Unit like the incident never happened. Standing in front of C-Unit the two watched as C.O.s and medical staff rushed to commissary.

"Nigga you a fool, who you think you is, Leon Spinks?" Sinica laughed but YaYo didn't see shit funny.

He had a life sentence and would be damned if he let somebody test his gangsta or manhood and Kanas Curt had done both. "Whatever, nigga, but check it out, my mans about to touchdown with some more tobacco. You trying to grab some?"

"Yeah, what he wants for a pouch?" Sinica asked.

"I'm paying one-hundred and forty books."

"Alright that's a bet, I got the books on deck, just let me know when you ready, my nigga."

"I'm a holla at you after chow time," YaYo said and walked in his unit.

After putting his commissary in his locker, he walked over to the phone and dialed his wifey's number. Shakira always answered YaYo's call, no matter where she was or what she was doing. She anticipated his daily calls.

Shakira was at the beauty salon doing a client's hair when her cell phone vibrated on her Gucci belt. After seeing it was her baby daddy, she politely excused herself from her client to take the call.

"You have a call from a Federal Correctional Institution, to accept this call press, 5."

Shakira pressed 5 with the quickness. "Hey, baby, I miss you," Shakira cooed into the phone.

"What's good, mami? I miss you, too, I'm just calling to hear your voice."

"I'm at work, right now, I got like four appointments today, it's packed.

"That's what's up ma get that money hustla. You want me to call back later?" YaYo asked as he eyed C.O., Ms. Sanchez walking past.

Ms. Sanchez had just started working Unit C-1, she was Mexican with long black silky hair and a body like the porn star Pinky.

"No, baby, I can talk about what's good?"

"Shakira, I really need to see you and Shamira. I thought I could hold off until I got transferred to a spot closer, but I can't take it no longer. I need to hug y'all, I need a visit, baby."

"Yaton I been telling you that, it's hard for me out here too, not being able to have you next to me when I wake up. I be lonely as shit."

"So, what you trying to say you need a nigga in the bed when you wake up? Because if that's what it is then shorty do you," YaYo said feeling insecure.

"See nigga that's what the fuck I'm talking about. You always flipping out on some dumb ass shit. I don't need a nigga in my bed. I need you, Yaton. *You!*" Shakira yelled into the phone getting upset.

"Shakira, I know you got needs, I got a life sentence. Just do you and don't have no other nigga around my seed."

Shakira looked at her cell phone like it had a flesh-eating disease before she pressed end on the phone terminating the call. A tear fell from her eye as she leaned up against the wall. The responsibility she had raising a daughter single-handedly was unbearable even with the help of Karen and the rest of the family. Shakira's life was taken away the moment the judge sentenced YaYo to life in prison. Her whole life was work and parenting, she didn't have a social life and with her being loyal to YaYo and a mother to Shamira sometimes burnt her out. She walked over to the sink and splashed some cold water on her face to bring her back from her emotions.

"Shakira, be strong everything is going to work itself out." She coached herself before going back to finish her client's hair.

YaYo was in his cell laying on his bunk thinking about Shakira. In the last couple of months, she had been acting a little different. A lot of times she was real short with her words and conversation and kept mentioning that she was lonely. On top of that, she was beginning to be more defensive when they talked about certain things. He loved Shakira with all his heart but he knew it would be hard for her. By him having a life sentence he knew it was over and one day she would find somebody else and move on with her life. YaYo understood the game, prison was the consequence for the way he lived his life, he had played the game, *and lost.*

YaYo played the game like a gangster and stood up to adversity, so therefore he took it on the chin like the boss he was. The only thing he felt he could do was keep his faith in God and pray to keep his family together. YaYo was stuck in his thoughts when somebody knocked on his cell door. He looked up and saw that it was BD, Pook.

"Come on in, fam," YaYo said motioning for Pook to come in.

"What you doing, killa?" Pook asked walking over to the window looking out at the yard.

"Shit what's up?" YaYo said up on his bunk.

"What you in here smoking on? I got two books. You trying to get high?"

"What kind of question is that? You already knew where the shit is at," YaYo said

Pook went in YaYo's locker and got the rolling papers, sat at the table and started breaking up the weed.

"I saw you over there arguing on the phone. You and wifey, good?" Pook asked with genuine concern for YaYo.

"Man, I don't know, bro, but I ain't with all that stressing shit she got going on. I'm trying to get her to be strong, right now she on some weak shit."

Pook used the two batteries before he sparked up the joint he finished rolling, taking a strong pull and exhaled the smoke through his nose. "Yeah, already know how I feel about that type of shit, my nigga. You gotta live and focus on you while you're in here. Focus on your situation. Get in that law library and work on your case. Nigga, you got a cop on your case who got indicted for corruption and all that type of shit, not to mention the main witness is nowhere to be found. Nigga if you get a new trial you can smash that shit and get that life off your back." Pook passed the weed to YaYo as he blew out a thick cloud of smoke.

YaYo hit the weed and let his mind ponder what Pook had just said. He had to find a way to get another trial and with ambition and drive, he would surely find a way. YaYo and BD Pook smoked a couple more joints and chopped it up until four o'clock count was called. YaYo sat in his cell formulating a plan, first thing in the morning he was going to the law library to holla at MR. B, the jailhouse lawyer.

S. Allen

CHAPTER 8

"So, you mean to tell me Shorty and Dave got whacked for going on a move I sent them on?"

"Yeah, chief, it's a young nigga block named, Quavon. He is supposed to be getting money on the Southside but got some people on Troy Street, so he put some dope on the block and now it's pumping. Say the lil' nigga got snipers on the roof with choppers and that's how Shorty and Dave got bodied," Buck one of Dave's workers confirmed.

"Oh yeah?" Top Cat said rubbing his grey goatee. "I like how shorty rocking. The way he got the shooters on the roof lets me know that he knows how to think. What you say his name is again?" Top Cat asked taking a pull from his Cuban cigar.

"His name is, Quavon. He's supposed to be, YaYo's younger brother."

"You talking about the leader of the G.B.C and how they got down in the streets." He had heard a lot of honorable stories about YaYo and had always respected his G just off what he heard.

"Listen up and listen carefully, bring him to me unharmed within the next twenty-four hours." Top Cat eyed the young soldier through bloodshot eyes resembling Lucifer himself. "Bring him to me."

"I'm on it chief," the soldier replied and left out the front door to carry out the orders that were given.

It was 3:30 in the afternoon and Quavon was at the Ford City mall doing a lil' shopping. It was Friday night, the King of Diamond's strip club was supposed to be popping and the place to be. Quavon had been at the *Lark* fashion store checking out a 3500 dollar *Michael Kors* leather jacket, he was about to purchase when his cell phone sprang to life. Looking at the caller ID seeing it was his mother, Karen, he answered.

"Hello," Quavon spoke into the phone as he passed the stack of bills to the exotic looking cashier who was eyeing him like he was a piece of chocolate.

"Where are you at, son? I just ordered some Curt's chicken and was wondering was you coming over."

"Yeah, ma I'm on my way over there. I gotta get dressed so I'll see you in about an hour."

"Okay, baby see you in a bit and be safe."

"Love you, ma."

"I love you, too!"

Quavon ended the call and decided to spit a lil' game at the cashier and try to get her numbers which were an easy task. After leaving out of the store with one of the freshest leathers in the city and Messhia's number, Quavon walked out the front entrance of the mall toward his new BMW X5. Quavon had to ditch the charger after he put in the work on Troy Street so he dropped fifty bands on the beamer truck. He had just started the whip with the remote starter when two black Range Rovers pulled up in opposite directions. The doors flew open and three masked men jumped out pointing choppas at Quavon. Quavon froze like a deer caught in headlights as he thought of reaching for the .40 on his waist. One of the gunmen musta read his mind and came over and snatched the Glock off him. Then without warning the gunmen brought the weapon down on top of Quavon's head knocking him out. Then threw him in the back of one of the SUVs and the two vehicles sped off burning rubber making a left on Western Street.

Top Cat sat in the comfort of his Mansion in a suburban area south of Chicago. The Richard Milli that surrounded his wrist read 9:15. The inside of Top-Cats Mansion was immaculate, the 8 bedrooms, 9 baths of 12,00 square feet was purchased with ten million dollars, worth of dope money that the Westside had bought him. He also had a mansion in Vero Beach Florida and at least six different condos throughout the city of Chicago. He wanted to be the biggest Heroin dealer in the Midwest and his recipe for wealth was simple murder and having the best product.

The way Quavon had his block set up reminded Top Cat of the 80s and how the original gangsters moved, that's why Top Cat wanted to persuade Quavon to be on his team. An enforcer like Quavon would have Top Cat on top of his game. The opportunity

44

to manifest his vision would be manageable with Quavon on the team and he knew it. As he saw the headlights of vehicles pulling into his circular driveway, he knew his goons had returned. Top Cat let a smile plaster his face as he went to let his men in.

****

Shakira had just tucked Shamira in bed and was sitting on the couch flicking the remote when she heard her doorbell ring. She stood up and stretched before she proceeded to her front door. It was 9:30 at night and she was interested in who was ringing her bell at this time, she wasn't expecting any visitors. She looked through the peephole and saw T.B. standing on the other side of the door with a quarter length mink on and a black skull cap covering his dreads. Shakira opened the door and let him in.

"Hey, T.B., what brings you over this time of night?" Shakira asked with her hands on her hips.

"My fault, Shakira, I didn't call first. I had this lil' bread on me, so I was trying to get it to you so you can send some to YaYo and pay a few bills," T.B. replied taking off his mink coat, putting it on the couch.

The diamonds that hung from his neck were so clear they looked like frozen ice cubes sitting on his black T-Shirt. His Burberry Cologne graced the airwaves inside of Shakira's living room. He walked over to Shakira's dinner table and placed two wads of cash on it.

"T.B. how much money is this?" Shakira asking picking up the money, fumbling through the fifties and hundreds.

"It ain't nothing much shorty, it's ten stacks." I see you got your hair done? It looks good on you," T.B. said touching the layers on Shakira's head with the back of his hand.

Shakira took a step back. "T.B. I told you, you don't have to be giving us all this money."

"Shakira, I know I don't have to do it, but I want to do it. YaYo's, my lil dude," T.B. said downsizing YaYo's status. "Plus, you a special person that deserves the finer things in life. A woman of your magnitude should be cherished and pampered. You loyal and you have a glow about yourself that even motivated me to be a better man. I wish and pray for a woman like you to walk into my life. You are one of the most beautiful sisters to grace my vision."

Shakira was speechless never had another man besides YaYo made her feel weak in the knees. Not to mention T.B.'s 6'1 frame, caramel complexion and boss demeanor made her moist between the legs.

T.B. knew he had Shakira by the lust in her eyes, so he moved in for the kill, pulled her toward him by the waist and kissed her, to his surprise Shakira kissed him back. Her nipples hardened inside her laced Victoria Secrets bra as T.B.'s dick stiffed threatening to bust through his Armani jeans. The two sampled each other's tongue before Shakira broke from T.B.'s embrace and pushed him off her.

"T.B. you need to get your coat and get out," Shakira said with her head down feeling bad for what had just happened.

"You right lil' mama, my bad." T.B. put on his coat and made his way to the front door. When Shakira stood with her hands on her hips. He stopped and looked deep into her brown eyes. "Shorty, I know I'm outta bounds but on some real shit I done caught feelings for you."

"T.B., get out!" Shakira yelled full of emotion.

T.B. walked out of Shakira's crib headed towards his Benz truck and heard the door slam behind him. He smiled, the damage had already been done, the seal to Shakira's heart had been penetrated. She was vulnerable and he was going to capitalize on it. He had always wanted Shakira for himself but YaYo was in the way. Since YaYo was in prison for life, T.B. had got his weight up in the streets and was now the chief of the G.B.C. in his mind. Quavon was ten toes down with the G.B.C. but it was T.B. who had gotten the Heroin connect that allowed the G.B.C to compete in the streets. T.B. wanted Shakira for himself. He had just tested Shakira and she failed in his book. T.B. jumped in his truck and pulled off into the night.

Shakira sat on the other side of the door crying her eyes out. She had just crossed the line and she knew it. T.B. had left her in tears, with a wet pussy. She needed to find a way to get T.B. off her mind. Shakira got up and walked over to the table where the stacks of money laid. T.B. was a baller and no matter how much she loved YaYo he wasn't there. She had grown to love T.B. as a person. For the last three years, T.B. had made sure that she and her daughter wanted for nothing. She had a nice condo on the Northside that was paid for, owned two cars and her daughter went to the best daycare and had everything a young child could want, it was all because of T.B.

Shakira without a doubt was attracted to T.B.'s swag. His money made him flourish into a boss and his gangsta kept niggas in line. She knew T.B. had elevated in the game and that alone attracted her to him. Her heart was pulling her in two directions, and she had to make a decision that would possibly change her life for better or worse.

****

Quavon sat tied to a chair with a pillowcase over his head and his hands tied behind his back. Three armed guards stood by with guns drawn on him ready to down his ass if he flinched the wrong way.

"Take the pillowcase from over his head," Quavon heard somebody say.

When the pillowcase was lifted off his head Quavon saw an older man in an all-white linen suite. His fingers and wrist were flooded with diamonds lighting up the dimly lit basement he was being held captive in. He looked to his left and saw a masked man holding a Tec-9, the 50 round clip made the weapon look menacing. When he looked to the right another goon stood on point with a DE trained at his rib cage.

"Untie him," the older man commanded and stepped closer to Quavon.

Quavon waited as they united the zip ties that had his wrist secured behind his back, he then stood up rubbing his wrist where the zip ties had broken his skin. Top Cat stepped closer to Quavon with his hand extended in greeting.

"Hello, Quavon, my name is Top-Cat. I have heard so much about you, it's an honor to meet you."

"Nigga, fuck you. Who is y'all niggas and what the fuck y'all want with me?" Quavon spat with ice on his tone.

"Quavon, what I want from you is your friendship. You killed two of my best soldiers. Now, soldiers can be replaced but leaders can't. And that's what I see in you, Quavon, a leader. You see Quavon, I run the Westside and not a nickel bag gets sold without my permission. You understand? Now so you can see I could have easily had you killed, but that would be such a waste of good talent." Top Cat took a pull from his Cuban cigar.

"You, niggas gone wish you'd killed me when me and my niggas come see y'all, better do your homework on me old man."

"Calm down, Quavon, I had you bought here to offer you a proposal of a lifetime."

"Oh, yeah, what's that grandpa? Just know your life's on borrowed time," Quavon sneered.

"Quavon, I'm offering you the chance to be Chief Enforcer in my organization. Soon I'm going to be running the Heroin trade in the city and the only niggas that are going to be able to eat are the niggas that's eating off my plate. The riches you will obtain from being my enforcer will be unheard of. Quavon, I have at least ten different spots doing no less than fifty gees a day in bags. You do the math, with you as my enforcer I would be willing to give you ten gees a day off each block you collect from."

"Man, fuck you and your blocks. Fuck you mean Chief Enforcer? Why would I want to be your Chief Enforcer and I'm the boss of my own squad?" Quavon laughed.

"Quavon, you have a lot of heart to speak to me with disrespect, but I can see us in the near future doing big things. So, if you want, you are free to leave. We will meet up again maybe next time on better terms, huh? I will have my men escort you to the front door."

"Yeah, that's what the fuck I thought," Quavon snapped zipping up his leather jacket.

Quavon was escorted to the front door. Once outside Quavon walked down the long driveway that led to the street. He saw a cocaine white *Mclaren 6505 Spider* that sat on custom 22-inch Lexani rims, also in the driveway was an orange *Lamborghini Gallardo.*

"Damn, this nigga got about a half mil in the driveway," Quavon said to himself. As he walked down the street, Quavon saw nothing but mansions and exclusive whips in the driveways. It was dark and he had no idea where he was. Quavon put his hand in his jacket to retrieve his cellphone but come up blank. "Shit," he yelled in frustration realizing that while he was being kidnapped, they musta took it from him. Having no other option, Quavon started walking back toward Top Cat's mansion to get his phone back.

"I'ma kill these niggas," Quavon said out loud as he banged on the large Oakwood door in front of Top Cat's mansion.

Top Cat opened the door with a shit-eating grin on his hardened face. "Back already, youngster?" Top Cat greeted and stepped aside, letting Quavon in.

Quavon brushed past Top Cat. "Man, listen old nigga I need my cell phone. Hurry up so I can come back and smoke you, niggas."

"Quavon, listen, why don't you have a seat and just let me speak? First and foremost, would you like something to drink?"

"Hell, naw nigga, I want my phone."

Top Cat motioned for one of his goons to go and get the phone as he walked over to his wet bar and grabbed a bottle of 1800 Tequila and poured two shots.

"Quavon, in this business it's all about networking. With my dope and your strategic muscle, we could rule the world and everything in it," Top Cat said and handed Quavon the shot of Tequila.

"From what I hear, Quavon your brother was a brilliant hustler who took a fall over a rat. Even with the rat testifying he still took the FEDs to trial and took his L like a real nigga. You are his brother and I can see that you share your brother's ambition and bloodline."

Quavon had just downed the shot of Tequila when one of the goons came back and tossed him his iPhone. The smooth liquor seemed to calm Quavon's nerves. "Where the fuck I'm I at?" Quavon hissed.

Top Cat gave Quavon the address to his mansion, not worrying about Quavon coming back to retaliate against him. Quavon sent a text on his phone as Top Cat continued.

"Quavon, I know you are a product of the G.B.C. organization and I respect that, but you are not a king, and I am willing to bring you to the table not just as my enforcer but as my partner."

"So, if you're willing to bring me in as a partner that means we're on some fifty-fifty shit, right?" Quavon asked.

"That's exactly what I'm saying, Quavon," Top Cat replied playing chess with Quavon's mind.

Top-Cat continued putting his game down for another thirty minutes until somebody started blowing their horn in his driveway. At the same time, Quavon received a text that read: //: *I'm outside.*

Quavon stood up and put on his jacket. "That's my ride, old school," Quavon said making his way toward the door.

Top Cat walked with him. "Quavon, just give it some thought and get back with me."

"Yes, I'll think about it," Quavon replied, walked out the door and got inside a Cadillac CTS.

Top Cat watched as the car made a left out of his driveway. The seed had been planted now all he had to do was sit back and patiently wait.

"Damn, boy who you know staying out here in these nice ass cribs." Tenesha a thick redbone Maniac asked from the driver's seat.

"Shorty, just get me the fuck away from here. It's a long story and I had a long day.

CHAPTER 9

"Maniac, you heard from Quavon, today?"

"Naw fam, I ain't hollered at him since yesterday. He was supposed to hit me up about a line he had on some Kush but he never got back with me," Maniac replied, putting an ounce of Heroin on the scale.

T.B. and Maniac had been hard at work for the last two hours breaking down and bagging a brick of dope. It was getting late and the two wanted to hurry up with the task at hand so they could hit the streets and drop off some weight to a few G.B.C members.

"That lil' nigga been acting fucky as shit the last couple of weeks. It's like all of a sudden he ain't coming around like he used to and he's killing me with this not answering the phone shit," T.B. said tying a knot on a 50-gram bag.

"Hold up let me hit this nigga's line real quick." Maniac picked up his Samsung Galaxy and dialed Quavon's number. The phone rang two times and went to voicemail. "It went to voicemail, bro," Maniac said and put the phone back on the table.

"I don't know what's up with that nigga but let's finish bagging this shit up and get this money. We'll get up with 'em sooner or later," T.B. replied.

The two gangsters continued to handle their business at hand when they finished, they left the trap spot to go dump off some work.

Quavon sat in the dark on a black sectional sofa in his mother's basement deep in thought. It had been three days since he was kidnapped by Top Cat's crew. Quavon had done a little homework of his own on the old head, Top Cat. He found out that Top Cat was a millionaire drug dealer that controlled most of the Heroin being pushed on the Westside of Chicago. Top Cat was the son of a millionaire gambler and Heroin dealer who went by the name, Flukey Stokes. When Top Cat was only fourteen, Flukey was gunned down in the streets of Chicago over a two-million-dollar gambling debt he owed. It was rumored that Flukey Stokes' Casket was made from a Cadillac so he was buried in a Cadillac Fleetwood as his casket.

Top Cat's vision was to exceed his father's legacy in the drug game and so far, he had been doing just that. Quavon also found out Top Cat commanded a M.O.B. of killers who he used to make sure his money was returned from off the streets. Those who come up short came up short in their lives. Quavon felt that Top Cat had tested his gangster by having him kidnapped. He thought about Top Cat's proposal. He knew Top Cat wasn't built like him or cut from the same cloth as him. Quavon looked at the prospect as a win-win for him and the G.B.C.

Once he penetrated his organization and his trust, he would then take over the Westside, the same side Top Cat claimed to be King of. In Quavon's mind, he wanted to run the whole city. If you sold drugs in the city of Chicago, you sold them for G.B.C and G.B.C only. It was either get down or lay down.

Quavon's phone vibrated inside his *True Religion* jeans and brought him out of his thoughts of Growth and Development. He glanced at the screen seeing that it was Maniac and sent him straight to voicemail. He didn't feel like talking to his homies, he hadn't even told them about him being kidnapped or about Top Cat's proposal. YaYo had always said that everything isn't for everybody. Quavon was a little stressed about the murder he'd committed on Troy Street. His first body was when he shot Butterball in which he felt no remorse. Butterball had sent his brother to prison her life, so his death was dealt with a cold heart, unlike the body he caught on Troy Street, it wasn't over revenge, it was over protecting his drug turf.

Quavon had awakened out of his sleep a few nights seeing Shorty's brains leaking on the side of the curb. Demons were hunting him. YaYo told Quavon that you can't move dope in the Chi without catching bodies. The dope game and the murda game coincide and at that moment, Quavon knew his body count would grow. He continued to sit in the dark plotting and scheming. He had to play chess to the highest level. He was formulating a play that would leave him the only King on the board.

****

YAYO

Back inside U.S.P. Pollock YaYo was waiting for the 8:00 move to be called so he could go to the law library to holla at Mr. B the jailhouse lawyer. Mr. B was from Memphis Tennessee. He had two consecutive life sentences. Even with him not being able to free himself from the class of the Federal Government, he mastered criminal law and was known for helping other convicts find loopholes in their case. Mr. B did his time in the prison law library and when he wasn't working on law, he was on the unit working out.

"Charlie Unit to Charlie Yard, Education and inside recreation five minutes move," YaYo heard the move on the intercom and walked out of the unit en route to the law library.

After taking off his G-Shock watch and placing it on a small table, YaYo walked through the metal detector and exited the building. Every unit in the prison had a metal detector. U.S.P Pollock was so bad with violence that a lot of staff turned their heads to certain things. An inmate could walk through the metal detector and beep and keep walking out the door without the officer saying anything. Most officers just wanted to do their eight hours and return home to their families without getting stabbed.

Once YaYo walked into the library he noticed, Mr. B at the computer. The prison library at Pollock was everything but a library. The gangs and other convicts used the library for a meeting ground to discuss prison politics, make drug deals and gossip about what was going on the compound. Only a few of the inmates in the population took advantage of the computers and typewriters to work on their cases or other positive benefiting activities, and Mr. B was one of them. YaYo walked past a table that was occupied by a few *Sex, Money, Murder* Bloods. The gang seemed to be in a serious conversation.

YaYo walked past and went into the room where Mr. B was typing on the computer and approached him. "Excuse me, Mr. B?"

Mr. B looked up from the computer. "Yes, do I know you, youngster?"

"No not really, my name's YaYo, I'm on the unit with you on C-1. I just wanted to ask you a few questions, if you have time."

Mr. B had lived on the unit with YaYo but had never spoken a word to the young thug. "How can I be of assistance to you, my black brother?" Mr. B asked.

"Well, word on the compound is that you're the man to go to about this law shit. I got a flimsy case, the dirty cop put me in some bogus shit, then they turn around and indicted him on some extortion type shit. They used a rat to get on the stand and make up a bunch of lies, now the rat was found dead somewhere in my city. I know if I get a new trial, I can beat the charges they indicted me on."

Mr. B rubbed his bald head as he digested what YaYo had just said. "Where are you from?" Mr. B asked.

"I'm from Chicago."

"You were a drug dealer in Chicago?"

"Yeah, I guess you can say that me and my squad have the lock and key on the city," YaYo bragged.

Mr. B frowned at YaYo's antics before he spoke. "So, you were out there living in boyish ways, huh? Like so many of our young black men."

"What do you mean by that?" YaYo asked feeling offended.

"YaYo, do you know the difference between a man and a boy?"

"Yeah, a boy can only do what he's allowed to do. A man does what he wants to do," YaYo answered like he was saying something slick.

Mr. B let out a slight chuckle. "My brother, a boy dreams and tries to make real a fantasy life. A boy takes his money and bags the hottest clothes that money can buy, the boy gets into games, oh yeah, he likes games he likes to play games with other people and with himself. The boy's characteristics, get manifested in a later stage as he prides himself as being a player. A boy likes to hang out with a gang, he doesn't particularly like the gang either he just wants somebody to play with. It's not really that he is committed to the gang even though one day he might have to die for the gang. The flashy cars are just like a little boy on a tricycle who says: *little girl you wanna ride on my new bike*. I bet you had one of those fancy two-seaters with the loud system and you probably had a family of five."

"Nigga you don't know shit about me," YaYo said getting mad.

Mr. B continued ignoring YaYo's aggression. "A man is the total opposite. A man refuses to die even in the predicament. He learns only when he takes full responsibility for his actions. He uses prison as a thinking tank and read books to further his knowledge, he tackles real-life problems and finds solutions. Instead of playing cards, gossiping and selling drugs on the compound he exercises his mind, body, and spirituality and has a proper, preparation, to prevent poor performance mind frame. He doesn't boast about the life he lived on the streets. He plans and finds ways of never putting himself in the same situation."

"Man, what all this shit got to do with my case and you helping me?" YaYo asked.

"It has everything to do with your case because you have to make a change in your situation and the change starts with you," Mr.B said standing up pointing his finger in YaYo's chest. "My brother, if you don't change your lifestyle me helping you with your case, will be a waste of time because you will continue to let the cycle repeat itself. It's up to you, YaYo to take control of your life because if you do get set free the FEDs will be waiting for you to fall again."

YaYo listened to Mr. B, he didn't come to hear all of the Black Panther speech but what Mr. B spoke hit home for YaYo and he knew that Mr. B was right. He was tired of being in prison and wouldn't wish prison on his worst enemies. He wanted a better life for him and his family.

"Mr. B, I understand what you're saying, but I really need you to take a look at my case."

"YaYo, I can see in your eyes that you have the potential to become something great and help our race stop the cycle of prison and self-inflicted genocide. If you can promise me and be a man of your word, saying that if you are set free you will help our brothers and sisters stop the cycle these white folks got us in. Then yes, I will do all that I can to help you get back in court. If you cannot commit to that then no, I cannot and will not waste my time," Mr. B said waiting for YaYo to make a decision.

The ball was now in his court, YaYo thought about it for a minute. Since he had been in prison, he had been around so many young black men with years upon years of time to do. Over seventy-five percent of the population had life sentences, the prison was like a cemetery and the gravestone read: Pollock U.S.P. The thought of it alone made a chill run down his spine. The person that came to mind was his lil' brother. Quavon. It would kill him mentally if Quavon came through the doors of U.S.P Pollock with a life sentence.

At that moment and time, YaYo made a decision. "Mr. B, you get me out of prison and I promise on my daughter, Shamira's life that I will do all that I can to help our people put an end to what is going on in our black communities."

Mr.B scanned YaYo's eyes looking into his soul and found truth in the words the young gangster spoke. Mr. B smiled and extended his hand. YaYo shook Mr. B's hand.

"YaYo, get me all of your paperwork pertaining to your indictment when we get back to the unit. Let's see if we got a chance at getting another one of our strong black men back into society where we need you."

YaYo and Mr. B continued to talk for the next hour until the move was called for the inmates to return to their housing units. Mr. B and YaYo had just formed a new bond and a new friendship.

It was 12:30 p.m. and Yayo and Sinica were walking back from the chow hall on the way back to the unit. It was a blazing hot 103 degrees and the Louisiana heat was unbearable

"Aye fam let me holla at this dude real quick and see what's the business on this package," YaYo said to Sinica referring to the tobacco they were waiting on.

"That's cool, I'ma head to the unit it's hot as a bitch out here. I'm coming out on the rec move. You coming out?"

"Yeah, I'ma come out, I should have some good news on that work," YaYo said. The two gave each other dap and YaYo walked over to a short Mexican. "What's up compadre?" YaYo said shaking his hand.

"YaYo, what's good my black brother?' Huey said trying to sound black.

Huey was from Dallas Texas. He was a young Mexican who had dealt major weight throughout Texas before he got busted with one-hundred kilos of Cocaine coming across the Mexican border. Huey was a pure hustler, even in prison Huey managed to keep his hands on everything that touched the prison and regulated the compound with weed, meth, tobacco, and dope. Huey had shit on lock and was getting plenty of money as he dealt with all races on the yard. The only color that mattered to Huey was green. If your money was right, then Huey was your plug. Huey lived in B-1, he and YaYo got introduced through a mutual friend and once Huey saw how YaYo hustled on the compound, he started fucking with him hard and they made plenty of money with each other.

"So, what's good Huey? You know a nigga ready to get it in. What's it looking like in the bag I ordered?"

"Well, my friend you want the good news first or the bad news?"

"Man, here we go with this bullshit. Give me the bad news," YaYo said becoming irritated, he hated playing games especially when it came to the money.

"Well, the bad news YaYo, is I couldn't get the whole order in. The good news is that I got half the order and I should have the other half this weekend within two days from now. I got that half on me, right now. So, what's good, my nigga?" Huey said.

YaYo had spent a thousand dollars with Huey and was supposed to get ten bags of tobacco which were equivalent to a pound and instead he was only going to get five pounds today. He knew how it went in prison and everything didn't always happen as shit was planned. He had been doing business with Huey long enough to know that Huey wasn't a bullshitter and never put shade in the game.

"That's cool, Huey. Listen the C.O. that's working my unit don't know nobody so you can sneak in the unit so we can take care of the business."

"Alright lead the way my friend," Huey said and the two walked to C-Unit.

Once in the unit YaYo and Huey went up to YaYo's cell. YaYo covered the window and went in his locker to grab a roll-on deodorant, taking the top off he used to measure the tobacco. They pulled out a Ziplock bag containing the product. YaYo weighed up all the tobacco, satisfied with the quantity he shook Huey's head.

"Like I said my friend no later than Sunday you should have the rest of your package."

"Alright, my nigga, I ain't tripping," YaYo said as they walked out of the cell.

Thirty minutes later YaYo was on the yard with Sinica walking the track. Sinica paid YaYo for two bags of tobacco. YaYo told him about the situation with Huey and how they had to wait a couple more days to get more, then he would be able to serve Sinica when he was ready to re-up. Sinica understood and was just happy to be getting something.

"So, what's up bro you get a chance to holler at, Mr. B about your case?"

"Yeah, I hollered at him this morning. That nigga on some real shit."

"As far as what?" Sinica asked.

"As far as getting a nigga back on them streets. The nigga made me promise if I get out to reach out to the young black youth in an attempt to help them get out of the hood, change their lives and move toward a more positive life. Show them a better way than dealing and killing."

"So, did you make the promise?"

"No doubt, man look around the fucking yard," YaYo said waving his hand around for emphasis. "Look at how many blacks it is than other races. I mean it's a few whites and a few Mexican but it's mostly blacks that populate this compound," YaYo said.

"So, how you gon' tell a nigga that's been surviving in the jungle all his life, selling dope and catching bodies to not choose that way to live? Them young niggas ain't trying to adhere to that shit, especially from a nigga like you who has left your fair share of blood on Chicago's concrete. You gonna sound like a hypocrite, YaYo."

"Man, one thing I know about young niggas is they gon' follow and listen to the nigga who got the money and influence. All we gotta do is school them on a new legal way to get money."

"I see, Mr. B done got in your head with that Black Panther shit," Sinica joked.

"That nigga just gave me something to think about fam. I started thinking about my lil' brother, Quavon. I don't want shorty walking through these gates of hell and walking the track like us for the rest of his life. That lil' nigga already out there falling in my footsteps.

"Yeah, I hear you family, this ain't no place to be straight up."

The two continue to walk the track chopping it up until the deuces went off, C.O.s and medical rushed out of the East door running towards A-Yard to stop an inmate-on-inmate assault. Three Bloods were jumping on another Blood.

"Alpha bravo! Charlie yard, yard recall return to your housing unit! Return to your housing unit! Yard recall!" the officer yelled over the intercom shutting the yard down.

"You think we going on lockdown?" Sinica asked as he and YaYo made their way back to C-Unit.

"Naw we should be good as long as they don't put the knife on 'em. Look like they were just kicking his ass."

"Good cause we don't need no lockdown, I got money to be made."

"Me too!" YaYo retorted.

They gave each other some gangsta dap and made their way through their housing unit. YaYo went straight to his cell and start bagging up some cigarettes. It was a lot of money on the compound and he was definitely trying to get it.

S. Allen

CHAPTER 10

It was 6:30 in the evening inside Pollock prison. YaYo was in the unit inside one of the two recreation rooms shooting dice. Each unit had two recreation rooms that were used for exercising. When inmates weren't exercising most of the time, the room was used for other activities, gambling was one of them.

"Bet two books I bet," YaYo said shaking the two, red-dice in his hand.

"You ain't said shit," a convicted pimp by the name of Moe-Rasy said and threw two more books of stamps into the pot.

"I bet four books you don't hit your point!" Smoke instigated betting against YaYo, dropping his money on the floor.

The more they betted against YaYo the more excited he got. He had been on a roll and the eighty books of stamps at his feet confirmed it.

"Bet nigga your money good to y'all niggas sweater than bear meat. Blacker than crew feet. Nigga point made," YaYo sneered and rolled the dice.

The crowd watched in awe as the red-dice slid across the floor, one dice landed on a two as the other dice continued to spin. In all, there were ten books of stamps brewing in the pot, one-hundred dollars in prison money.

"What size rims I had on my Chevy, sixes?" YaYo yelled.

The other dice landed on a four, Black and Smoke put their heads down in defeat all while. YaYo picked up his winning with a grin on his face. YaYo was in the midst of trash-talking to the losers when all of a sudden, they heard inmates banging on their windows.

Boom! Boooom! Boooom! Boooom!

YaYo went to his cell to look out the window to see what all the commotion was all about. A bus had just rolled in and that meant a slew of new inmates were being released to the compound. YaYo saw at least twenty inmates walking with the C.O.s to their assigned housing units. Scanning the faces looking for anybody familiar he found none. After seeing none of the new inmates were coming to his unit, C-1, YaYo decided to go back in the rec-room to finish punishing the dice game.

After shooting dice for another thirty minutes. Yayo heard the C.O. yell, "Chow!"

He picked up his stamps, went to his cell to go and stash them and headed out of the unit for dinner. When YaYo walked out of the unit Sinica and Pook stood waiting for him.

"Man, I just punished them goof ass niggas for one-hundred and twenty books. That shit sweet in there," YaYo bragged.

"Oh, yeah, I'm glad you got some books cuz a nigga needs a loan," Pook said joking with YaYo as the three of them made their way to the chow hall.

"Aye YaYo they said one of the guys just got off the bus, he a G.D. from Chicago," Sinica informed.

"What's his name?"

"He says his name is Wild-Wild. Say he from the hunnids and just came from U.S.P. Hazelton."

"Where he at?" YaYo inquired.

"He should be in the chow hall."

When the three gangsters walking entered the prison's dining room YaYo saw the new nigga that Sinica was talking about. The dude was brown-skinned with tattoos covering his face making him have a goonish appearance. The guy looked familiar to YaYo but he couldn't put a finger on his familiarity or where he knew him from. After getting their trays they went to the table and took a seat. YaYo was sitting directly across from Wild-Wild, who kept a mean mug on his face as he continued to eat his chicken. When he and YaYo made eye contact, YaYo was the first to speak.

"What's good, fam? My name's YaYo, 69th and Walcott."

"I'm Wild-Wild," the thug replied not even looking up at YaYo. "You from Chicago?"

"Yeah, I'm from Chicago. I'm from the hunnids, 111th Street."

"Oh, that's what's up." YaYo started putting salt and pepper on his chicken.

Once YaYo got finished eating he got up to dump his tray with Sinica, Pook, and Wild-Wild in tow. While walking back to the unit Wild-Wild was hollering at Sinica.

"Aye, fam, you Sinica from 119th and Wallace, right?"

"Yeah, that's me. What's the bizness?"

"Man, my nigga I heard a lot about you throughout the system. Niggas say you push that knife. I was locked up with Goon and 'em in Victorville, California ?"

"Yeah, that's my nigga, he butchered a nigga down there. A Carolina nigga -- fam a straight goon."

"You was down there with Mateo too, huh?" Sinica asked.

"Yeah, I was down there with that clown. That's how I ended up getting transferred I smashed his bitch ass."

YaYo and Sinica looked at each other with perplexed looks. "What other joints you been to?" Sinica probed.

"I been to U.S.P Atwater."

"Van was down there in, Atwater with you?"

"You talking about Van from Homan & Ohio? Yeah, he was down there until we ran his bitch ass up off the compound. I busted his ass, too," Wild-Wild replied.

"Damn, fam, you like putting your knife in the guys, huh?" Sinica asked him with a mug on his face.

"Well, you know you got good men and you got evil men. This FEDs shit all fucked up. Niggas have a lil' power on the yard and be trying to use that shit to exploit the guys. I don't be with that shit. So. I'll let my knife speak for me because niggas don't understand how law but they understand that wet work," Wild-Wild replied breaking down his logic.

Sinica shook his head in disagreement. "The homies you stabbed was good niggas—my niggas."

"It is what it is fam. Just know all calls were made righteously." Wild-Wild had a lil' smirk on his face.

Pook and YaYo walked in the unit leaving Wild-Wild there by himself.

"Man something up with that nigga. It's something about him, I guarantee we gon' end up running his ass up, watch," YaYo told Pook as they walked through the metal detector and into the unit.

"Well, one thing about it, and one thing for sure this ain't Victorville. This bloody Pollock and if his ass gotta go he ain't going walking, he's going bleeding," Pook said meaning every word, ready and willing to assist YaYo in any righteous endeavor.

The next day YaYo was on the yard by himself doing burpees. He had a lot on his mind, Shakira was one of them. Ever since their lil' argument, she had not picked up the phone and that alone had YaYo vexed. He had emailed her, and she hadn't even emailed him back. YaYo told himself that when he got back in the unit he was going to email his lil' brother Quavon and tell him to swing through to go check on Shamira for him.

YaYo tried not to worry about Shakira and what she was out there doing but that was easier said than done. Shakira had proven her love over and over to YaYo and he didn't understand why he was having the negative insecure thoughts about their relationship. He knew he was a thorough bread nigga but carrying a life sentence on your back was a different kind of beast. He wasn't prepared for the mental challenge that was bestowed upon him and it was now all starting to take a toll on him.

YaYo's thoughts and exercise were interrupted when Sneezy and Wild-Wild walked up. Sneezy was one of those fake gossiping cats who could never seem to stop his mouth from running. He and Sneezy had words a few times and each time when YaYo called him to the cell for some work, Sneezy would always duck rec and want to talk it out. To get out the gangsta shit. Ever since Wild-Wild had gotten off the bus, he and Sneezy had been on some buddy shit because of the work they had been in Victorville California together.

Then it hit YaYo like a ton of bricks, it was Sneezy who had shown YaYo prison photos and pointed out Wild-Wild in the pic saying, "This Wild-Wild, he stabbed like five of the guys and ain't shit happen to him. My nigga a straight monster," Sneezy would brag, dick riding like the true dick rider he was.

YAYO

YaYo felt in his heart that trouble was brewing as he continued doing his burpees.

"YaYo what's good, homie?" Wild-Wild said taking off his shirt revealing all his prison tats.

"Ain't shit, what's good homie?" YaYo grabbed his towel off the ground to wipe the sweat from his face.

"So, you the YaYo that was running the G.B.C? I been off the streets for ten years but you know a nigga keep his ear to the streets. They say y'all niggas was out there getting the bag. How much time the FEDs throw you?"

"I got a life sentence, my nigga," YaYo said trying to keep his convo short with the U.F.O.

"Damn, my nigga, that's fucked up. You new to the FEDs so I'ma put you up on some game. It ain't the other cats you gotta worry about clashing with, it's always the homies. You gotta keep your knife on you at all times, cuz you never knew when a nigga gon' try and bring you a move," Wild-Wild said with sinister intent in his tone and facial expression.

Sneezy had a big smirk on his face now back activated with the dick riding shit.

"Well, I ain't got no beef with none of the homies and my paperwork straight, so I ain't worried about a nigga bringing me a move," YaYo replied pulling his T-Shirt over his head.

"Word on the pound is you the one to holla at if I was trying to get some tobacco. What's up? Put a nigga on my G."

YaYo couldn't believe what he had just heard. Wild-Wild hadn't been on the compound forty-eight hours but yet he already knew his business which only meant that Sneezy had been running his mouth to Wild-Wild about what was going on, on the yard. YaYo put nothing behind the nigga Sneezy, he had probably even given the nigga Wild-Wild a knife. YaYo answered his own question when he saw the imprint of a bone crusher in the pocket of Wild-Wild's jogging pants. Protocol for the guys was you had to have your paperwork cleared before you could hustle on the yard or be armed. YaYo was a stand-up nigga and didn't deal with the trivial games.

"Aye fam what's up with your paperwork?" YaYo asked.

Wild-Wild gritted his teeth before he said, "Nigga my paper-work in my property and when it gets here I'ma present it. Best believe I'm straight."

"Well, when you get cleared come holla at me about getting some money," was all YaYo said as he picked up his water bottle and walked off to go do some pull-ups, leaving the two clowns standing there.

YaYo looked over his shoulder and saw them mean-mugging him as they talked. He knew at that moment that Wild-Wild was going to be a problem. He made a mental note to watch Wild-Wild and the moves he was making. Once back in the unit YaYo went to the computer to send Quavon an email.

What's good, lil bro? Me I'm cool just need you to do me a lil' favor. I need you to slide by Shakira's crib and check on her and Shamira for me. She ain't been picking up the phone or emailing me. I hope you out there being safe and moving with caution? This federal shit ain't living. I love you!

YaYo sent the email to his brother and made his way to his cell to gather his things to get in the shower when he ran into Mr. B.

"Peace my brother, YaYo. What's going on?"

"How are you, Mr. B? I was just about ready to jump in the shower. What's up?"

"Well, I was looking over your motion of Discovery and I must say that you were involved in the streets something serious. They already have you being the head of a Criminal Organization. That tells me that you have a major influence over a lot of black men in the city of Chicago. Meaning that you have a mind to captivate other minds. Imagine if you used that talent for good instead of evil? You could be the next Malcolm X or the next Doctor King." YaYo took the compliment on the chin, as Mr. B continued.

"YaYo, or can I call you Yaton?"

"You can call me, Yaton, Mr. B."

"Well, Yaton, I have found a few loopholes in your case but I'm telling you right now that this fight is not going to be easy. These are not state charges these charges were brought down by the United

States Government but we are going to do all that we can to get you a new trial. If we can get you a new trial, you will have a seventy-five percent chance of getting out."

YaYo couldn't believe what he was hearing. It was a possibility that he could give the FEDs back the life sentence that was given to him. "Mr. B, I appreciate what you are doing for me."

"No don't thank me with your words. Thank me with your actions, by getting out and holding up your side of the bargain," Mr. B said.

Mr. B and YaYo talked for another five minutes before YaYo went off to get in the shower. Mr. B had just given him the morale he needed. It had been dark and now Mr. B had just given YaYo the light in the tunnel.

****

Three Weeks Later

"Aye YaYo somebody at the door for you!" A dude named Rude-Boy yelled up to YaYo's cell.

YaYo was in his cell with Pook debating about who was thicker *Nicki Minaj* or *Cardi B*. "I'm fucking with, Nicki," YaYo said walking out of his cell en route to the front door. As he walked up he saw Sinica with a serious expression on his face.

"What up with you, nigga? A nigga on your ass?" YaYo joked.

"Aye, bruh, fuck all that goofy shit. Come outside to the yard, on the next move it's important," Sinica said with murder in his eyes.

"Alright, fam. You good?"

"YaYo just come outside, I'ma holler at you about it when you get to the yard. And bring your knife, too." Sinica walked off leaving YaYo with his adrenaline now rushing.

YaYo went up to his cell and grabbed both of his six-inch bangas and concealed them in his jogging pants, something was definitely about to pop off. The 1:30 p.m. move was called. C-Unit had

C-Yard. When YaYo got to the yard he saw at least four of the homies including, Sinica.

Sinica waved him over to where they were posted. "What's up, YaYo?" Sinica greeted.

"What's up?" said O.G. Ed.

Skateboard greeted YaYo with a head nod the same as O.G. Patches. All the men in attendance were the shot-callers for the Chicago car.

O.G. Ed spoke first, "YaYo, that nigga, Wild-Wild gotta go. We just received an email from the higher up saying that he has a green light on his head, he's hot."

A small smirk came across YaYo's lips because he had a feeling about Wild-Wild from the first day he'd met him.

"That nigga got eighty years. The FEDs still gave his rat ass three-hundred and sixty months, stupid motherfucker," O.G. Patches intervened.

"YaYo, since he's in you and Sinica's unit we need y'all to orchestrate his removal. We don't want y'all to participate in the move, just orchestrate it and make sure it's carried out right without any of the homies getting hurt," Skateboard laid out the orders to the soldiers.

"Just know YaYo that this killer rat is known for stabbing the guys for trying to run his hot ass up. So, make sure that shit don't happen on this yard. You understand?"

YaYo nodded his head to the big homies acknowledging the mission and the orders that were given to him. Sinica had a smirk on his face like he was the cat that swallowed the canary. Just the thought of violence made his dick hard.

The O.G.s walked off after giving the orders to be carried out leaving YaYo and Sinica standing there.

"Man, who we gon' get to do this shit?" Sinica asked ready to get shit cracking.

"We ain't gon' get nobody to do it. We gonna do this shit, me and you. I didn't like that nigga from the jump. Now we find out he a snitch. This his last night in Pollock because in the morning he going to the infirmary," YaYo said ready to put in work.

"How you want to do it, on the yard or in his unit?" Sinica asked as he and Yayo started to walk back to the unit.

"When that nigga come back from that workout class, he takes in the morning I'ma already be in y'all unit waiting on his ass. When he goes in his cell, we gon' run up there and crush his ass and let the C.O's find him."

YaYo knew Wild-Wild's daily routine and knew that in the morning Wild-Wild would be attending a workout class with a Texas nigga named, Six-Five.

"How you gon' get out of the unit after we blast his ass?" Sinica inquired.

"We gon' hide his ass under the bunk until they call the move for chow, then we gon' slide out and go eat with the rest of the unit. Tomorrow's Wednesday—Burger and French fries, can't miss that," YaYo replied like it was nothing.

"Nigga, you ever push that knife before?"

"Nigga, I been bleeding niggas since I was a kid. Sit back and just watch me work," YaYo replied with a smirk.

"We gon' show the B.O.P why they call this bitch bloody Pollock," Sinica vowed.

****

The Next Morning

The next morning Wild-Wild was on his way back to his unit with the Texas cat Six-Five. On the way, he ran into his man Sneezy.

"Wild-Wild, what's up my nigga?" Sneezy yelled like Wild-Wild was Young Jeezy and he was his biggest fan.

"What's good, bro, what you got going on?"

"Ain't shit I was trying to see if you were trying to get some weed. This Memphis nigga got some caps for like fifteen books."

"Oh, yeah, is the nigga sweet?" Wild-Wild said thinking on some crud ball shit.

"As a baby's ass," Sneezy replied.

"What on, A-2?"

"That's a bet, my dude. You already know how we was doing it in Victorville, strip a nigga down to his draws and take all that shit."

"After lunch we over there," Sneezy said with a shady look on his face.

The two criminals walked back up C-Unit, Sneezy went in C-1 and Wild-Wild walked up to C-3 both excited about the lick they had set up after chow.

Wild-Wild came into the unit and went to the computer to check his email. After seeing he had none, he made his way upstairs to his cell to get his shower things ready. While in his locker grabbing his hygiene items he was alerted when his cell door swung open. When he turned around, he was greeted by a white flash from being punched in his left eye. The two intruders that invaded his privacy had on grey skull caps and towels covering their faces. Wild-Wild tried to ball up to protect himself from the blows that were being inflicted upon him. Then he felt a cold piercing pain enter his back.

"Hot ass nigga," YaYo said through clenched teeth as he repeatedly stabbed Wild-Wild in the back, head, and arm until blood stained the floor inside the small cell. Wild-Wild let out a helpless scream as Sinica stabbed him in the side of his jaw with the bone crusher knocking out three of his teeth puncturing his jawline.

"Bitch ass nigga you think that shit a game?" Sinica sneered.

Wild-Wild had been stabbed many times and lost so much blood that he passed out. The cell reeked of freshly spilled blood as YaYo and Sinica pushed Wild-Wild's unconscious body under the bunk barely breathing. YaYo looked down at his blood-stained clothes and knew he didn't have a chance of getting past the C.O.s with all the blood he had on him. He went in Wild-Wild's locker, took out a pair of tan khaki pants and changed his clothes, Sinica followed suite. The two goons changed clothes and waited for the chow move to be called while Wild-Wild laid under the bunk bleeding profusely.

Once the move was called the two slid out of the unit dumping their bloody clothes in a trash can on the way out, undetected. While in the chow hall, YaYo had started putting ketchup on his burger when C.O.s and Medical staff started running towards C-Unit. YaYo heard the call come over a walkie talkie on an officer who was standing close by.

All officers to C-Unit, C-3 inmate unresponsive, I repeat C-3 inmate unresponsive."

Sinica looked up at YaYo and winked like the crazed lunatic that he was. YaYo had just lost his appetite, at that moment he prayed a silent prayer. Praying that he didn't get caught for what he had just done.

S. Allen

CHAPTER 11

"Girl for real, I know you love your baby daddy and all but you can't let, YaYo keep stressing you out. He got a life sentence and you're out here by yourself—with a baby," Candy said.

Shakira and her best friend Candy had been on the phone for the last hour and a half. Shakira was stressed out over the argument that she'd on the phone with YaYo, not to mention T.B. had been coming at her extra hard and she was confused as to where her loyalties stood with, YaYo. So, she vented with her BFF.

"It's like he be questioning me about shit out the blue. I told him I was lonely and the nigga straight flipped out on me, talking about *if I want to do me then go ahead and do me*. Girl, I was mad as hell when he said that corny shit," Shakira replied as she flicked through the channels on her 70-inch plasma.

"Did you tell him about his boy coming at you?"

"Girl, hell no, if I told YaYo about that shit he would really be flipping out. He'd probably send somebody over here to kill me and T.B.," Shakira said as a joke but was dead ass serious. Just the thought alone caused a chill to go down her spine. She knew her daughter's father did not play no games.

"Shakira let me ask you a question, do you have feelings for T.B.?"

"Candy, I don't really know what I feel for T.B. He has been here for me and my daughter since YaYo been locked up and to be honest it's because of him that me and Shamira want for nothing."

"Well, all I can tell you is that life is real short and you shouldn't have to put your life on hold because YaYo has a life sentence. Because unless they overturn his sentence some kind of way, you will never have the life you want with him anyway,"

Shakira let what her best friend was saying ponder in her thoughts. She loved YaYo with all her heart and soul and would want nothing more than for him to come home so they could be a family, but the chances of that happening were slim to none and she knew that. Thinking about being with T.B. would go against everything that she stood for and that was Loyalty. Shakira was one with

YaYo and his family. Karen, Davon, Quavon, and Honey. What would they all think about her, they would definitely see it as betrayal knowing how much, YaYo loves her and his daughter. Shakira knew she had to stay away from T.B. and his advances because in all actuality she was becoming attracted to his presence.

Candy broke her from her thoughts. "Girl, you know they got this new club that just opened in Milwaukee Wisconsin it's called, *Dream.* It's supposed to be popping this Friday night, let's slide through there," Candy said changing the subject.

"I don't know girl, I do need to get out of this damn house and get my mind right. I don't know if I can get a babysitter though."

"Why don't you get Karen to watch her?"

"I guess I can ask her."

"That's what I'm talking about bitch lets go kick it. My friend Tamika from work can come with us. You know it can be a girl's night out," Candy said excited as hell.

"We'll see Candy, I'll call you later this week and let you know for sure."

The girls continued talking for another fifteen minutes before they ended their call.

"You know maybe a girl's night out might be what I need," Shakira said to herself. Little did she know that one night out was going to put her life in a whole different swing.

$$****$$

Quavon was pushing his BMW X5 through the midday Chicago traffic. He was supposed to be in a Physics class but instead, he was headed to the Westside to meet up with Top Cat. School had become less and less of a priority. The way he figured it was he didn't need college, all he needed was the money he was obtaining from the drug game. He was becoming more and more addicted to the blue notes he was stacking and after being kidnapped, he decided to take the game to another level.

Quavon had phoned Top Cat and told him he wanted to meet up to discuss the business proposal, he and Top Cat agreed to meet him on Chicago Avenue and Pulaski Street. Quavon had thought long and hard about what he was about to get himself involved in. He had a vicious crew and the money G.B.C was touching was almost unreal, but Quavon wanted more and his thirst for power started to subside his being. Looking through the lenses of his *Cartier* Frame, his vision to put a vice grip on the streets of the Chi was about to flourish. The streets would now, and forever be controlled by the G.B.C.

The Westside of Chicago was a gold mine. There was a Heroin block on the Westside that did no less than $100,000 a day and Troy Street was a prime example of the riches that could be brought from the Heroin. The only thing stopping Quavon and the G.B.C from locking down the Westside was Top Cat and his crew of shooters. Quavon had failed to let T.B. and the G.B.C know what he was up to. YaYo had told Quavon years ago that when you are in a leadership position or position of authority you don't let your man know everything because everything ain't for everybody. Quavon was moving with the jewels his brother had given him. The games had just begun.

As he made a left on Chicago Avenue his phone sprang to life. He looked at the caller I.D. seeing that it was Top Cat, he answered. "What's good?" Quavon answered as he pulled up to a red light next to a Cocaine white Push Truck, the driver of the foreign was a sexy lil' redbone.

"Quavon, how are you? Where you at?"

"I'm at a light on Chicago Avenue, I'm about to pull up in two minutes. Where do you want me to meet you?" Quavon asked.

"I'm at the restaurant Jimmy's on Pulaski, pull in the parking lot. I'm in a black Escalade. What you in?"

When the light turned green the driver in the Porche truck blew Quavon a kiss and sped off. Quavon smiled as he spoke into the phone. "I'm in a BMW X5 on twenty-fours," Quavon replied with cockiness in his voice.

"Youngster I see you have exquisite taste. When you pull up jump in the backseat and we will spin a few blocks," Top Cat said and ended the call.

Another two minutes later, Quavon was pulling into Jimmy's parking lot. He parked on the side of the black Cadillac Escalade, grabbed his Glock 19 from under the driver's seat and concealed it on the waistline of his *Givenchy* jeans before hopping out his whip. After activating the automatic alarm, Quavon walked over to the Escalade and got in the back seat. When he got in the truck Top Cat was sitting in the back smoking a Cuban Cigar with a bottle of Rose Black between his legs. An older bald head brother occupied the driver's seat.

"Quavon, my good brother. Thank you for coming to meet me. Benny hit a few blocks would you?" Top Cat said to the driver.

"Alright Chief," was Benny's only reply before he started the SUV and pulled the expensive vehicle into the hustle and bustle of the streets of the Chi.

Quavon looked over at Top Cat and noticed the clear diamonds that surrounded his neck and the carats that flooded his wrist with ice. The *Ferragamo* suit he was rocking looked to cost thousands. Top Cat poured Quavon a shot of the Rose Black and passed him the drink. After pouring a shot for himself, Top Cat downed the smooth liquor, savoring the taste.

"Ummmh, only the best for the best." The warm liquor warmed his chest. "So, Quavon, I see you have thought about what we discussed since our last encounter?"

"Yeah, I thought about it." Quavon downed his shot of Rose.

"So, what's it gon' be youngin'? You gon' assist me in ruling these streets or you gon' let the streets rule you?"

Quavon grinned before he spoke, "Man, listen old school I ain't no minor or do boy. I got my own shit going on out here and I got a team of head bussas at my beck and call. So, how can me being the enforcer in your organization benefit me and my niggas?"

"Quavon, first and foremost, I respect you and what your family has built but understand that times have changed drastically. You see, Quavon, when I was your age I was just like you. I had an undying hunger for money and I still do, don't get me wrong. When I went to state prison in the eighties I did my bid by myself which left me bitter to the ones who left me for dead in the belly of the beast.

The ones that never wrote or ever sent me money for a bar of soap that only cost dollars, it made me bitter to the world. I made a vow to never put myself in that situation ever again. The only thing that solidifies a man in this world is if that man is a ruler of his own destiny, Quavon, I have a thirst—a thirst for complete dominance in these streets. The only way to achieve complete dominance is through fines, precision and networking with the right individuals and that's where you come into play," Top Cat said pouring another drink.

"So, if you got all this shit, what the fuck you need me for?"

"To look over and command the soldiers in my organization, Quavon. I have a plug so good that I could flood these streets for the next twenty years with the purest form of Cocaine and Heroin. But I need an enforcer of your heart and capabilities to keep the soldiers in line. As you know in my organization or drug crew there are rules and laws that must be upheld in order for the organization to move forward. If you know this, then you know there will be those who will go against the grain and break laws and policies. My laws and policies. As my enforcer, it will be your job to detect the individuals and pursue their proper punishment as you see fit. You also know that a man of my status wears a crown, and in this game, there can only be one king." Top Cat looked Quavon in his eyes trying to read his thoughts on the words he had just spoken.

"So, now that I know my staff titles and duties. What's my paper gone be looking like?"

"Quavon, you handle your function like I know you will. I will be willing to pay you one-hundred and fifty grand a month. After you have proven your loyalty to me I will bring you all the way in and have you sitting next to me on the throne. No less than fifty-fifty."

Quavon rubbed his freshly trimmed goatee like he was in deep thought, in all actuality he had already had his plan laid out now all he had to do was execute it. Top Cat had tested his gangster by having him kidnapped. Quavon was from the same bloodline as YaYo. YaYo had fallen and now it was time for Quavon to rise. This was his opportunity to set his name in stone in the concrete of Chi-Raq.

Quavon was about to have the streets in his clutch with impeccable supremacy.

"What's it going to be, youngin'?" Top Cat asked.

"I accept your proposal only on one condition."

"What's that, Quavon?"

"You let me handle my business the way I handle it. You just sit back and keep the dope coming and let me run these streets."

A huge smile spread across Top Cat's fat lips. "You have a deal with my brother. Let us have a toast. Money, power, and respect."

"And Murda!" Quavon added.

CHAPTER 12

Two days after the meeting with Top Cat, Quavon was parked in the parking lot of Kennedy King College waiting for his twin brother, Davon to get out of class. Top Cat had given Quavon the layout on his Heroin operation, giving him the route in which the money was to be collected. Quavon would be responsible for picking up $460,000 daily. Almost half of million in drug money from the drug blocks on the Westside. Standing now as the chief enforcer for the crew all lieutenants and security personnel answered to him and Quavon answered to nobody but Top Cat.

Since taking his position of authority, service had already mentally started to reconstruct the operation to his liking. First, he would revamp the security format on each of the blocks, give promotions and demotions. Each block would open up shop at 5:00 a.m. on the dot and shut down at precisely 9:00 p.m. At 9:00 p.m. the workers would have given the days earnings to the block lieutenant, then Quavon would pick up the money for Top Cat, shorts would be unacceptable and punishable by death. Quavon had been given the authority to run Top Cat's operation and he was going to do just that, with an iron fist. Penetrating the operation was going to be easy, as the plan had already been laid.

Quavon saw Davon coming out of the front doors of the small community college. Quavon was proud of his twin brother. He didn't lose track of school by the money, drugs, and women that surrounded him. Davon was focused on school and making something out of his life. He would always say that he was going to do something big in the graphic design field, and one day he would be rich and pay the government to let YaYo out of prison. A smile spread across Quavon's face as he thought about his twin. Seeing that his brother didn't notice what car he was in, Quavon beeped the horn three times to get his brother's attention. Davon looked, saw Quavon sunk low in the seat of the X5, walked over to the car and got in the passenger seat.

"What's up, bro, who car is this?" Davon asked looking around the spacious foreign whip. The smell of new leather invaded his nostrils.

"Who sitting in the driver's seat nerd brain?" Quavon joked pulling out of the parking lot of Kennedy King College.

"When you get this pretty muthafucka?"

"A few weeks ago. You know a nigga had to grab something to give these suckas something to hate on," Quavon replied switching lanes.

"Yeah, I see you, but on the real, I see you haven't been going to class. What's up with that shit?" Davon asked putting his back-pack in the back seat.

"Bro, you already know that school shit ain't for me."

"Goofy ass nigga, you only got one more year before you grad-uate, now you about to drop out. Please make that shit make sense."

Quavon sighed. "Listen, Davon, you finish school and let me go this money out here. Then I'ma put all this street money into you getting a big business started with that graphic design shit. That's how I'ma clean my money. We gon' be eating, bro."

"Man, I can get a loan from a bank or something. You ain't gotta risking your life or freedom out here so I can start a business."

"Nigga you talking about a weak ass business loan. Davon, I'm talking about millions of dollars. I can see it, bro, it's in my clutch, I just need you to graduate and I'ma take care of the rest," Quavon said pushing the X5 on the Don Ryan Expressway.

"I don't know, bro, I just don't want you out here like that. I don't need you to end up like, YaYo. Plus, what is mama and granny gon' say, about you dropping out of school and shit? That's gonna crush mama and you know it."

"First of all, I'm not gonna end up like Yaton. YaYo had too much trust in too many different niggas, that's how he got ratted out. I don't trust no nigga, but you, that's the most valuable thing I learned from our brother. As far as mama, she already hip to what I'm involved in and I swear on a stack of bibles Davon, in the end, mama gon' be proud of me."

Davon stared out the window while silence engulfed the whip. After a couple of minutes, Quavon broke the silence. "Davon, are you with me or what?"

"Man, I don't like the way you're going about things with this *get rich or die trying shit*. But you my twin and I'm never against you. So, I guess I'm with you. Just promise me one thing, Quavon."

"What's that, bro?"

"Promise me you won't make our mama bury you."

"Davon, I promise you and everybody I love that I will not let these niggas kill me," Quavon vowed.

Davon looked at his evil twin before he said," Then I guess I'm with you, bro."

Quavon smiled at his brother, turned up the sounds and started bobbing his head to a *40 Gotti* track and got off at the next exit to drop his brother off at the crib.

****

Shakira, Candy, and Tamika had just pulled in the parking lot at Club Dream in Milwaukee Wisconsin two hours away from Chicago. The parking lot was packed with exclusive vehicles from *Cadillac Trucks, Benzes, Camaros*, to *Dodge Chargers*. Shakira parked her *Lincoln MKZ* next to an *Ashton Martin VG* coup that was sitting on some 24s.

"Damn, girl these niggas in the Mill is getting some *M-O-N-E-Y!*" Candy yelled over the music playing in the car.

Milwaukee was basically a baby Chicago, coke and dope money flowed through the city like the Nile River. The niggas in the Mill reaped the profits of the profitable but deadly drug game.

Shakira had gotten Karen to watch Shamira for the weekend, so she was out just to have a good night out with some friends. After getting out of the car Shakira and her friend made their way to the entrance of the club.

"Damn, ma, I see you rocking them jeans. Can I go with you?" Shakira could barely make out the driver's face, all she could see was the diamonds that shined in his grill.

The dude had to be talking to her because out of the three of them she was the only one wearing jeans. Candy and Tamika wore short skimpy skirts that left nothing to the imagination. Shakira was killing them in her too tight *Prada* jeans. She had always been thick but after she had Shamira her ass protruded and was cut like two basketballs. Her *Jimmy Choo* pumps and matching handbag had her looking like the diva she was. Shakira politely smiled at the man in the Bentley and kept it moving.

"Girl, you is tripping. Why you ain't get that nigga number?" Candy said wishing she was the one the dude in the Bentley was talking to.

"Bitch, please! Get his number for what?"

"Cuz he in a Bentley, duh!" Tamika added her two cents, giving Candy a high five.

"Whatever," Shakira replied as they entered the club.

Club Dream was a big club, mirrors surrounded the entire club, the club had three floors and three different bars. The smell of high-grade marijuana was in the air as *Gucci Mane's Love for Money* featuring *Trey Songz* graced the airwaves. The niggas in the club were turnt up to the max popping bottles of *Rose* and *Ciroc*.

Shakira looked around the dimly lit club and said to herself, *"These niggas in Milwaukee getting to that bag."* She watched how the dope boys in the club were stunting and throwing money around. Shakira and her friends made their way to the bar to get some drinks.

"Excuse me, excuse me!" Shakira yelled over the loud music to get the bartender's attention.

"How can I help you lovely ladies tonight?" The bartender flashed a flirtatious, Colgate smile. He was a dark-skinned brother, athletically built, with a smooth baritone that had Candy lusting.

"Let us get three shots of 1800 and three Long Island ice-teas. "

After the bartender returned with their drinks, Shakira went into her Jimmy Choo bag to pull out the money to pay. Just then, a dude with short dreads walked up. He was five-eleven, brown-skinned, with a confident stride to his walk and swagger that emanated from his pores. He wore an all-white *Pelle Pelle* outfit and the ice on his neck blinged bright enough to light up a dark cave. The charm on his necklaces was a box of arm and hammer flooded with clear diamonds. The guy went in his jeans and pulled out a ridiculous wad of money and peeled off a crispy blue face hundred.

"I got their drinks," he said with authority and passed the big face to the bartender telling him to keep the change.

Shakira stuck her money back in her purse. "Thank you," she said looking at the guy from head to toe. She was definitely impressed the smell of his *Gucci* cologne was doing numbers on her.

"What's your name lil' mama?"

"Well, it's definitely not lil' mama. If you must know my name is, Shakira," Shakira replied with an attitude, sipping her Long Island.

"Shakira, huh? That's pretty. They call me, Snow Man."

"*Snow Man*, what kind of name is that?" Shakira asked now downing her shot of Tequila.

"The kind of name that's connected to money," Snowman retorted with swag dripping.

"Well, nice to meet you, Snowman. These are my girls, Candy and Tamika."

Candy was looking at Snowman like she wanted to suck his dick right there in the middle of the club. Snowman was ordering the women another round of drinks when his two homies walked up smoking a blunt of loud.

Snowman introduced his goons. "Aye, y'all these my homies, Doe-Boy and Cutter. Y'all wanna roll up to the V.I.P. with us, so we can show y'all how we do it in the Mill?" Snowman asked, not waiting for a reply as he grabbed Shakira's hand leading her to the V.I.P. section of the club.

As they walked up the stairway to the V.I.P, Shakira could see that the V.I.P section was cracking. It was big, had large leather sectional sofas around the room and was occupied by ballers, popping bottles and smoking fat blunts of Kush. Half-naked women sat on their laps or were cuddled up, trying to find a way to get some of the drug money that was being thrown around. When Shakira and the rest of the crew walked into the V.I.P., she couldn't believe who she saw. Sitting on the couch dipped in Diamonds with a bottle of Hennessy in his hands was, T.B. and some of the G.B.C. gangsters.

'*This has to be a coincidence,*' Shakira thought. She was about to turn around.

T.B. noticed her and yelled her name. "Aye, Shakira!" T.B. yelled and stood up and started walking toward her. "Shakira, what you doing up here? And who the fuck is this clown, ass nigga?" T.B. said mean-mugging Snowman.

"Who the fuck you calling a clown?" Snowman stepped towards T.B.

"T.B., chill you don't tell me where to be or who I can talk to," Shakira said stepping between the two men.

Menace and Bootyman got up pushing the sac-chasers that were sitting on their laps to the floor and rushed over to assist T.B.

Doe Boy and Cutter stood on side of Snowman, ready to get active.

"Don't tell me you out of town niggas trying to get slumped over a bitch? You know where the fuck y'all at? This Killwaukee," Snowman sneered.

Shakira rolled her eyes and snapped her neck at the same time.

"Who the fuck you, calling a bitch?" Shakira said feeling disrespected.

"You, bitch!" Snowman said with ice in his tone.

At that moment shit got real, T.B. brought the Hennessy bottle across Snowman's face, as Menace produced a pocketknife from his *Robin Jeans* and stabbed Cutter in the kidney. Doe Boy seeing the drama unfold and the blood that was being shed knew they were outnumbered, so he ran out of the V.I.P trying to get to the trunk.

T.B., Menace, Bootyman and a few others G.B.C gangsters stomped Snowman and Cutter unconscious, punishing the fake thugs with bottles and chairs until the lights came on in the club and the bouncers rushed toward the V.I.P. T.B. was still in a zone stomping Snowman's head to the floor when Menace pulled him off him.

"Come on fam let's get up outta here." T.B. came back to reality, out of the zone he was in. He grabbed Shakira by her arm and the rest of the G.B.C made a frantic exit out of the club leaving their victims as casualties to gangsta shit.

Outside the club, T.B. ushered Shakira toward his Benz Truck.

"Uh, T.B., I drove here with my girls I don't need a ride."

"Well, you can tell your girls that you're good. You can get your car in the morning," T.B. commanded hitting the automatic start button on his keychain.

"Why I gotta ride with you for?"

"Shorty, just get in the truck," T.B. answered while Milwaukee police swarmed the parking lot.

Shakira walked over to where her girls were standing and handed Candy her car keys.

"What's these for?" Candy asked looking at the keys in her hands.

"I'ma ride with, T.B.," Shakira said.

Candy smiled at her. "Girl, that's what I'm talking about. Gone and get your back broke in. God knows you need it."

"It ain't even like that, he's just giving me a ride."

"Yeah, whatever bitch call me in the morning with details."

Shakira was about to respond with something slick until gunfire erupted in the parking lot.

Boc! Boc! Boc! Boc!

Doe Boy let the .45 rip in the air, clearing out the parking lot. Club goers ran in different directions in an attempt to get to their vehicles. T.B. pulled up in his truck honking his horn. Shakira hopped on the passenger side and T.B. pushed the gas speeding out of the chaotic parking lot.

S. Allen

CHAPTER 13

It was 3:30 in the morning as Quavon rode through the city in deep thought. He had a lot on his mind. He'd taken Top Cat up on his offer but for his own personal benefits. He knew the game he was playing would lead him to the top of the drug game or his demise. Quavon was going to finish what his brother YaYo started, and that he was adamant about. Thinking about his brother reminded him that YaYo had asked him to slide through Shakira's crib to check on her and Shamira, and let her know that YaYo was trying to contact her.

He looked at the time on his iPhone and saw that it was extremely late, but he figured since he was already on that side of town he would stop through just to make sure his family straight. Fifteen minutes later, Quavon turned his BMW down as he pulled onto Shakira's block on the Northside of Chicago.

As he pulled up to her condo a sneer came across his lips when he saw T.B.'s Benz truck in the driveway. *That's why you ain't been hollering at bro, huh?* Quavon killed the lights and parked on the side of T.B.'s truck, he reached under his seat, grabbed his .40, stuck it on his waist and got out. Somebody had a lot of explaining to do.

Shakira sat on the opposite side of the couch from T.B. The whole ride back from Milwaukee he had been trying to pursue Shakira into being with him. She was confused, she loved YaYo with all her heart but YaYo wasn't there. T.B. kept repeating to Shakira that YaYo had life and was never coming home, just the word *life* made her heart hurt. She didn't want to be alone for the rest of her life. It made her mad because she was constantly trying to get YaYo to leave the streets, now he was in the FEDs with *life* and she was starting to resent him for that.

T.B. sat on the couch in his wife-beater smoking a blunt of Sour Diesel. The way he was staring at Shakira through the red glossy eyes made her feel wanted as she returned his lustful stare. T.B. put the blunt duck out in the ashtray, got up and walked over to Shakira. He pulled her close and planted a soft kiss on her forehead. Shakira's heart began to beat fast and T.B. had felt it. He grabbed her voluptuous ass cheeks, squeezing them while sliding his tongue in her mouth. Shakira kissed him back, she had let her guard down as her pussy started throbbing.

While they were engaged in passionate lip lock the doorbell rang.

"Who the fuck is that?" T.B. asked mad at himself for leaving his FW in the truck.

"I don't know." Shakira was nervous as who was at her door three something in the morning. She got up to go look out the peephole. When she saw Quavon on the other side of the door her heart stop.

"Oh, my God," was the only thing she could say as she put her head down. She had no choice but to answer the door.

"Who is it, shorty?" T.B. said putting on his sweater.

"Quavon," Shakira mumbled.

"I knew this was a bad idea. T.B. just get your stuff and leave. I don't want no drama, please just leave."

The doorbell rang again, she had been caught. As T.B. was zipping up his coat, Shakira opened the door and Quavon walked in.

"Damn, fam, my big bro in the penitentiary sleeping on a concrete slab and you out here sleeping in his bed?' Quavon said confronting T.B. on his disrespect.

"It ain't even like that, Quavon, I just gave Shakira a ride from the club that's it," T.B. said telling only half the truth.

"Alright, I appreciate it fam. Now I guess you can bounce, it's kind of late don't you think?"

"Hold up shorty who are you speaking to like that? Better check your tone when you're speaking to me."

"Nigga you heard what the fuck I said," Quavon said checking T.B.'s gangsta.

"I think you better stay in your lane, shorty. You're fam lil' brother and all, but if you ain't know, I'm Chief of the G.B.C. You better show some respect."

Quavon turned his face to the side and let out a slight chuckle. "Chief of the G.B.C., huh?" Quavon pulled his Ruger off his waist and put it in T.B.'s face.

"What you gonna do with that? I'm supposed to be scared cuz you gotta gun? I know one thing you better bust that motherfucker, because if you don't next time I see you I'ma make you eat that bitch," T.B. said looking down the barrel of Quavon's .40

"Please, would y'all please stop it," Shakira pleaded.

"Yeah, that's what the fuck I thought. Nigga you ain't on shit." Quavon pulled the slide back on the Ruger putting one in the chamber. "Out of respect for my brother's baby mama nigga, I'm not gon' melt your shit. You clown ass nigga, but next time I might not be so respectful. Get the fuck up outta here."

"You gon' wish you ain't pull that motherfucker, Quavon. Trust and believe when I see you again, I'ma make sure I show you the same gangsta you on now." T.B. walked past Quavon toward the front door. When he walked past Shakira, he stopped and wiped the lone tear that escaped from her emotions. He smiled and said, "I'm holla at you later, ma. Everything will be all good." He turned back to face Quavon mugging him with a mask of murder. "And I'll see you in the streets, shorty," was all that was said before T.B. exited the front door, hopped into his truck and smashed out.

"So, this how you do my brother, huh? He in the FEDs and you out here messing with his right-hand man?"

The tears started to flow down ShaKira's cheeks. "It's not like that, Quavon. I swear he just gave me a ride from Milwaukee."

Quavon just shook his head in disbelief as he walked toward the front door. Then he stopped and said, "My brother been worried sick about you and Shamira. My advice is that you get in contact with him and let him know y'all straight."

Shakira nodded her head in understanding. "Quavon!"

Quavon turned around to face Shakira. "Are you going to tell, Yaton about this?" she asked.

Quavon looked at her like she was crazy. "What kind of question is that? Of course, I'm gon' tell him," he retorted and left her standing there pending in her guilt. Quavon was heated leaving Shakira condo.

He couldn't believe that T.B. out of everybody would be the one to betray YaYo not the G.B.C by coming at YaYo's girl. YaYo had always preached to him the importance of loyalty. Quavon had looked up to T.B. since he was a youngster, T.B. was basically family. YaYo and T.B. were close as thieves and had put the G.B.C organization into a lucrative empire. Quavon knew that by him pulling his strap on T.B. and not killing him, T.B. would want his head served on a platter. He knew he should have shot him but what was done was done and he would have to deal with it.

Quavon knew that some would side with T.B. while others would side with him. It would be a war within the M.O.B he would have to crush T.B. and whoever was riding with him and he was going to use Top Cat's men to do it. For his young wicked mind, he started to formulate a play that would make him the King off the throne. It was now time to stake his claim in the streets and his position to be known to all who oppose him. The streets were about to scream bloody murder and everybody far and near was going to hear his voice.

****

Back Inside U.S.P Pollock

It had been two weeks since YaYo and Sinica brought Wild-Wild the vicious move that sent him to the infirmary. The prison was on lockdown status due to the incident. The warden of the prison had threatened to leave it on lockdown because nobody was apprehended for the assault. The video surveillance showed nothing, and Wild- Wild even if he wanted to snitch was in no predicament too. Word on the yard was that he got hit twenty-six times and was pronounced dead on the scene. He was rushed to the hospital by air flight. Luckily the doctors and medical staff were able to bring him back to life and he was now in an intense coma.

YaYo felt different since the stabbing, he was a nervous wreck. Every time officers came on the unit, he thought they were coming to snatch him up. A new case would definitely mess up his chances of getting back in court. He still hadn't heard from Shakira, he'd sent two letters since the lockdown and haven't received anything back. He knew Quavon would check up on them, and when he did, he would let him know.

YaYo was reading an Urban Fiction Novel by *Eddie Wolf* called, *A Dope Boy's Prayer* when his celly hopped off the bunk.

"Mmm, what's good, Yayo?" You been acting real strange lately like you got something on your mind heavy," Paco said and grabbed some crackers out his locker.

YaYo laid the book on his chest. "I ain't on shit just reading this book. This shit like that."

"Come on, my nigga, I been in the cell with you for three years. I know you better than anybody," Paco said and got back on the bunk.

"Naw fam, I'm good"

"You probably thinking about that work you and your man put in?"

YaYo sat up. "What are you talking about, Paco?" YaYo asked. He'd never told Paco about what he and Sinica had done to Wild-Wild, so he was starting to wonder where he got the information from.

"YaYo the whole penitentiary knows y'all crushed that nigga in C-3. Niggas just ain't snitching. That's a good thing because if niggas was talking like that you would be in the S.H.U. by now, straight like that."

YaYo just shook his head still not admitting to anything.

"For real YaYo you need to chill the fuck out if you're trying to get back to them streets. Before you fuck around and catch a body in here and get some more time. I know a lot of people that wish like hell they had the chance you got. Feel me?"

"Yeah, I know, I can wait till they let us back up so I can get up with Mr. B. I'm starting to feel like this prison is turning me into some kind of savage."

"Fam you been a savage, it's just this place and the condition bring shit outta niggas. You gotta contain your demons and humble yourself. That's the only way you're gon' make it around here."

YaYo knew that Paco was right. He had damn near just caught a jailhouse murder on some send-off mission. He definitely needed to get his priorities in order if he ever wanted another shot at his freedom. He had a daughter to look after, he would be damned if he let prison and its politics stand in the way of that.

YaYo and Paco continued to converse about life and freedom when the C.O. slid a piece of paper under the door. YaYo got off the bed and read the memo and smiled.

"What it say, YaYo?" Paco asked in anticipation.

"We coming off lockdown in the morning, my nigga!" YaYo was happy.

The sooner they got off lockdown the sooner he could get to the law library with Mr. B, get to working on his case and walking the path that would lead to his freedom.

CHAPTER 14

Quavon slid through the Westside in a tinted Ford Taurus. Occupying the passenger seat was one of Top Cat's henchmen who went by the name of Roccett. Roccett was a rolling 20s Crip from the Eastside of Atlanta Georgia. He was Top Cat's sister's son. Roccett stayed in trouble in the streets of the 'A' so his mother begged her brother he let him come to Chicago to help raise him because Roccett's father had been in prison his whole life. Top Cat knew his eighteen-year-old nephew was wild and played with them pistols and could use his violent tactics in the streets of Chicago. Roccett knew the Westside and all the drug blocks controlled by Top Cat and for that reason, he paired him up with Quavon, so Roccett could show him the lay of the land. At first, Quavon was against the help but in a short time found Roccett useful. He liked Roccett's serious demeanor and the young thug never asked questions, he just followed orders.

Quavon and Roccett were en-route to one of Top Cat's drug blocks to pick up some money. It was early in the day and he and Roccett had a lot of moves to make. As they pulled up on Averas and Thomas, the block seemed to be pumping with action, dope fiends waited in a single file line to get served some of the best heroin the city had to offer. After parking in the middle of the block in front of a three-story building, Quavon and Roccett stepped out of the whip and walked to the front of the building where a small crew of gang members stood.

"What's good, player?" One of the thugs greeted.

Quavon ignored the dude and made his way inside the building headed to the second floor. Once Quavon found the apartment he was looking for he banged on the door three times. Loud music could be heard coming from the other side of the door as pungent weed smoke escaped from under it. Noticing nobody coming to the door, Quavon banged on the door again with more force.

"These niggas think shit's a game. Every time we come through here it's the same shit," Quavon said visibly angered.

From the other side of the door, the music was turned down. "Who is it?" A voice yelled from behind the door.

Quavon was irritated. "Nigga open the fucking door," Queven said through clenched teeth.

The sound of the deadbolts being unlocked could be heard from the other side. "My fault, big homie. Didn't even hear you knocking," Cheeseburger said stepping to the side to let Quavon and Roccett into the apartment.

"How the fuck you gon' hear me knocking if you got the music all the way up, dummy?"

Inside the small apartment was four other gangster smoking weed and playing a video game on a large television. Cheeseburger remained standing in the doorway.

"Man, why the fuck you standing there looking stupid? Go get that money!" Quavon was getting more and more irritated being in the presence of these clowns. Cheeseburger hesitantly went to the back room and returned with a black Nike duffle bag. Quavon yanked the bag from Cheeseburger and unzipped it. "How much is this?" Quavon asked as the money looked short.

"It's thirty stacks."

"*Thirty stacks*? Nigga it's almost two in the afternoon and all y'all niggas made is thirty punk-ass stacks?"

"Shit moving kinda slow today. Shit like that some days. Top Cat, ain't tell you that?'

Quavon took Cheeseburger's sarcastic remark as a challenge and had to put him in his place. "Motherfucka I ain't gon' ask Top Cat shit. If y'all get out on the block and grind instead of playing video games all day you might meet it. Matter fact since you wanna be smart, when I come back through here on the last pick up. If lt ain't another seventy thousand in this bag I'ma fuck you up," Quavon snapped directing his threat to Cheeseburger.

One of the goons on the couch looked at Quavon with a sinister facial expression Roccett feeling the tension coming off the couch pulled a large chrome revolver from the front of his army fatigue cargo pants pulling the hammer back.

"Aye shawty! You got a problem with what the homie speaking?" He aimed the large pistol at the dude who had the animosity.

The dude shook his head now scared to death from the sight of the Cannon.

Quavon continued, "Like I was saying, have that paper right when I slide back through here."

Quavon and Roccett left the apartment and got back to the task at hand, picking up Top Cat's money.

****

T.B. sat at the head of a large table in the back of Foxy Lady's bar on 119th and Halsted. Sitting around the table were a few head G.B.C members.

T.B. stood up to address his gang. "I want to thank y'all players for coming down here tonight. The reason I asked y'all to attend the meeting is to discuss some major issues. There are going to be some major changes starting today. First and foremost, Quavon is eradicated from G.B.C. as of right now, I'm sanctioning a green light on his head, he is now an enemy of the people."

Whispers could be heard amongst the men.

"On what grounds?" Menace questioned. Menace had been brought into the G.B.C by YaYo and had much love for YaYo and Quavon.

"On the grounds of insubordination. It was brought to my attention that, Quavon went to the plug in an attempt to make a play for himself and leave all of us stranded," T.B. lied.

"So, don't we have to take some kind of vote on this shit? That's YaYo's lil' bro," Menace questioned his authority but knew he had to keep his emotions in check and play this out like a gangsta. He knew nobody except him had access to the plug. Therefore nobody except him could verify this story.

"Naw ain't gon' be no vote. I'm Commander in Chief for G.B.C. This ain't no fuckery democracy. It's a dictatorship and like I said, Quavon gotta go." T.B. sneered his comment toward Menace. "Now this the business my niggas, we gon' get to this money how we been getting it. The plug says he gonna up the shipment by one-hundred more bricks. So, from this point, we gon' get two-hundred keys a month on consignment." The looks of greed could be seen on all their faces, except Menace's. T.B. continued, "My niggas it's time for us to expand G.B.C to an international force to be reckoned with. We are no longer a bunch of radicals. We are now the great whites of the sea. Let it be known that we will be at the top of the food chain. At the top, we will remain."

The bosses at the table erupted in cheer, except Menace, T.B. noticed immediately. "Menace, you look like you got something on your mind, care to share it with the rest of the family?"

"Naw everything cool, T.B.," Menace lied.

He knew something was fishy, T.B. had just green-lighted Quavon without the G.B.C hearing Quavon's side of the story. Menace could smell the bullshit. He had to get up with Quavon and fast.

An hour later the G.B.C was leaving the Foxy Lady.

"Aye Menace, I need you to drop me off at my lil' broad's crib on the low-end," T.B. said following Menace to his Jeep Cherokee.

"Don't trip I got you," Menace said really not wanting to fuck with T.B. right now.

As he drove down the Don Ryan Expressway Menace looked over at T.B. to fully reveal his hand about the Quavon situation. "Aye fam, what's really up with, Quavon?"

T.B. lit the tip of the blunt and took a long pull. "I thought I already explained that shit," T.B. said blowing smoke through his nostrils.

"It just doesn't seem like Quavon to be on some shady shit like that. That's all I'm saying."

"You know fam, money makes niggas do some strange, unloyal shit." T.B. passed Menace the blunt. Menace just shook his head at the bullshit T.B. was kicking. "Don't worry my nigga, we gon' be rich as hell in a minute, fuck, Quavon. Get off at the next exit."

Menace got off on 35th Street. After parking in front of the Stateway Project, T.B. inhaled the rest of the weed and tossed the roach out the window. "You know, Menace, the only thing a nigga can respect in life is loyalty. Without loyalty you have nothing, always be loyal to those that are loyal to you," was all that T.B. said as he pulled a 9mm and put it to the side of Menace's head.

Boc! He splattered blood and brain tissue on the driver's side window. T.B. used the back of his hand to wipe some of Menace's brains off the side of his face before he hopped out of the Cherokee leaving Menace's lifeless body in the whip as he escaped into the darkness of the poverty-stricken streets of the Southside.

****

It was the 12:30 move when YaYo walked through the Pollock law-library. It had been a long lockdown and he was glad it was over so he could get to his legal work. As he walked into the prison library a lot of other inmates gave him stares and head nods, a lot of what's up and respects. The word had got around the compound that YaYo was the one who put the work in and got the prison on lockdown. In a jungle where only the lions survive, being known to push that knife gave you an aura of respect amongst the predators, YaYo had just earned his.

YaYo saw Mr.B at the computer and approached him. "What's up, Mr. B?"

Mr. B acknowledged YaYo greeting without looking up from the computer screen. "Mr. Anderson, how are you? I see you really not trying to get to the streets, are you?" Mr. B said not looking at YaYo.

"Why you say that, Mr. B? I brought my paperwork just like you asked," YaYo said not knowing where Mr. B was coming from.

"Yaton, have a seat." Mr. B nodded his head to the empty seat beside him. YaYo hesitantly sat down next Mr. B. "Yaton, I'm having a hard time trying to figure you out. You come to me asking me for help. I give you my word as a man and as a convict that I would do all in my power to help you in your situation. Then you go and stab somebody or allegedly stab somebody. Now I have been on lock for twenty-five years and trust and believe I know how things go in these penitentiaries. Sometimes you gotta do what you gotta do, but something is telling me that you had a choice and could have avoided the incident. I may be wrong, but all I'm saying is you gotta get your mind out of this prison and its politics and focus on the bigger picture. That's getting out and staying out. Always remember, Yaton, your homies will use you until they can't use you anymore. Then when your services are no longer needed. They will do you how y'all did that boy in C-3. Trust and believe me when I say you gotta worry about you and your situation."

YaYo was thinking about what Mr. B was saying. He knew that Mr. B was speaking the truth. He had a choice. He could stay involved with prison politics or focus on the bigger picture, getting back to his family. YaYo nodded his head in understanding.

"Now what you got there gangsta?" YaYo passed Mr. B the yellow manila envelope.

"That's my trial transcript."

Mr. B began looking through the paperwork. "I'm going to go through your transcripts and see what loopholes we can approach. Once I find them I'm going to the start filing motions to get you back in court to address those issues. I'm letting you know, right now, Yaton that things like this don't happen overnight. It's going to take patience, let's remember that we are dealing with the FEDs but we can beat them. Understand this, at any time I feel you are not taking this seriously, and you are wasting my time. I will return your things and it will be over. You understand?" Mr. B was serious as a heart attack.

"You got my word, Mr. B, I will get my shit together," YaYo said truthfully.

"Remember, Yaton, a man's word is his bond."

CHAPTER 15

Quavon stood in a kitchen in one of Top Cat's dope houses overseeing the manufacturing of Heroin. Seven naked women with surgical masks sat at a table mixing and packing the drugs for distribution. One of Top Cat's soldiers named, Big-Bolo stood at the front door with a Mossburg pump. Quavon wanted to know everything about Top Cat's operation. So, he was hands-on with all the action. He wanted to be precise about the layout of the land. So, when the time came, he wouldn't fail in his undertaking.

"Quavon, when you gon' let a bitch get a lil' taste of that hot dick?" A worker mixing drugs asked Quavon, out her lane.

"When you're able to tend to this dick shorty, but right now, you're worried about the wrong shit. Focus on what the fuck you're doing!" Quavon said coldly putting the workers in her place. The chick rolled her eyes but continued doing what she was doing, mixing the dope. Quavon's phone vibrated in the pocket in his *True Religion* jeans. He grabbed it, looked at the number and answered. "What's good, fam?" He listened for a minute, then replied, "What! When? Meet me on 49th, I'm on my way."

"Alright, we'll be waiting," said the caller.

Quavon ended the call.

Looking at his man, he said, "Bolo, make sure these hoes don't cuff nothing and close this shit down till further notice," Quavon commanded and rushed out of the trap house.

Quavon pushed his whip down the Dan Ryan Expressway. He couldn't believe the news he had just received about Menace's body getting found on the Southside. Menace was always on point, but he had so many enemies anybody could have been responsible for his murder. Quavon was on his way to meet up with some of the G.B.C members, Reggie 'G', Choppa and Crusha at the Robert Taylor Projects. If anybody had some information about Menace's murder the G.B.C would.

Quavon pulled up to the projects spotting Reggie 'G's Range Rover and Crusha's S class Mercedes Benz. Quavon parked on the side of the Benz and got out.

"What's good, Quavon?" Crusha said smoking a blunt of purple Haze.

Reggie and Choppa stood in front of the whip.

"Yeah, what's good with y'all?" Quavon shook up with his people.

"Lil' bro I think you need to bend the block with us. We definitely need to holla at you." Crusha was stone-faced.

Quavon looked in each man's face. He didn't know if they were trying to rock him to sleep or not. Shit was getting ugly in the streets and his trust level was low. One thing was for sure the .40 on his waist was trustworthy. Quavon got in the back seat of Crusha's Benz.

"Listen we gon' get straight to the point," Crusha said pulling out of the parking lot. "The nigga T.B. just put a green light on your head. He said you tried to cuff the plug."

"That's a lie," Quavon retorted from the back seat, now clutching his .40 as Crusha watch him through the rearview mirror.

"We already knew that fam," Reggie 'G' intervened.

"We think T.B. shot Menace. We left the meeting together and T.B. jumped in the car with Menace. He was the last one with Menace."

"That doesn't make sense, Menace is his man," Quavon said confused.

"You snatching the plug don't either."

"Man, this the business, Joe. That bitch ass nigga was at Shakira's crib at three in the morning when I pulled up. YaYo asked me to spin through and check on them. Me and the nigga had some words, and for his total disrespect for my brother, I upped the strap on him. He got to talking that chief shit and I wasn't going for it. I didn't know he'd come to y'all about me cuffing the plug. My niggas, I don't even know the plug," Quavon vented truthfully to his men.

"You know, Menace was taking up for you at the meeting, questioning that bullshit story, T.B. was spitting. And that's probably how he got knocked down." Crush was putting the piece of the puzzle together.

"What's up with the rest of the crew, how they feel about this shit?" Quavon asked.

"You already know, T.B. feeding them niggas, so they rolling with who got the bag. Bandaid, Joe-Joe, Murda, and Suicide on some dick riding shit."

"So, who y'all loyalty lay with?"

"We loyal to our Chief and that's YaYo, you his blood so it is what it is. We family nigga, blood over money," Reggie 'G' expressed who side he was on.

"You with us then we with you, just like that," Crusha said.

Quavon thought about the situation and if he could truly trust the niggas, he was in the car with. Crusha had been around from the beginning and was related to Pudge, YaYo's right-hand man that got killed a few years ago.

Reggie was like an Uncle to him, making sure he looked out for Quavon while YaYo was in the FEDs. Choppa got his name because his favorite guns he murdered with were Choppas, AK-47s, AR-15s, and Mac 90s, just to name a few. Choppa had been a designated hitter for YaYo so his spot within G.B.C was concrete. Quavon's heart told him he was in the company of some righteous G.B.C gangstas. At that moment he chose to bring them into the fold. The streets was about to bleed, Quavon and those loyal to him would reign supreme, those on the other side would be laid to rest.

Quavon proceeded to tell the G.B.C about the situation he had going on with Top Cat and his drug operation. The plan would unfold like the sweetest story ever told. The G.B.C. would take over the Westside Heroin track using calculated Murda and Strategic fitness, at the same time, Quavon would eliminate T.B. and his flunkies. At the end of the chess game, Quavon would be the only piece on the board.

After laying out his murderous plan to his squad Crusha dropped Quavon back at his car.

"Y'all just be ready to move on my beck and call," Quavon said and got out the car.

"Don't even trip lil' bro we stay ready, so we don't have to get ready," Crusha replied.

The seed had been planted. A war was about to ignite and only the strong would survive. It was now do or die.

****

YaYo had just walked into the unit from outside recreation. He was covered in sweat from the 300 Navy Seals he had just done and was in desperate need of a shower.

"Excuse me, Mr. Anderson you have a visitor," the C.O. Ms. Sanchez said eyeing him provocatively.

"Alright, Ms. Sanchez, I appreciate that," YaYo said and made his way to the shower.

YaYo's mind was running wild as to who was in the waiting room waiting to see him. He silently prayed that it was Shakira and his daughter. He still hadn't talked to Shakira and that alone had him perplexed. After getting out of the shower YaYo went back into his cell and a pair of creased, tan khakis, laced up his Jordan Retro 4's and using a hair tie he put his long dreadlocks into a ponytail. He had been growing his hair for almost four years, so it hung past his shoulders. After putting on some *Jimmy Choo* cologne that he had purchased from the commissary, YaYo was ready for his visit.

Twenty minutes later, YaYo entered the prison's visitation room. He scanned the visiting area for Shakira and his daughter but came up blank. Who he did see had him equally excited.

"What's good, young nigga?" YaYo said hugging his brother Quavon.

"Ain't shit big bro." Quavon broke YaYo's embrace stepping back to check him out.

"I see you looking good, all big and shit," Quavon said.

"Look like you out there doing real good for yourself?" YaYo responded noticing the clear diamonds that surrounded Quavon's neck looking like miniature ice-cubes.

YaYo and Quavon took a seat at the visiting table.

"How you doing, big bro?"

"I can't complain fam due to the current situation. How mama, granny, and Davon?"

"They doing good bro, everybody sends their love and respects. Ma busy with work and Davon on his school shit about to graduate." Quavon put his head down, he had been dreading the question the whole plane ride.

"What about Shakira and my baby."

Quavon told YaYo what he needed to hear. He told him about T.B. and how he caught him at Shakira's house at three in the morning. He told YaYo about how T.B. had sanctioned a death violation on him. Quavon gave his brother all the details about Top Cat and the situation that was going on with that. YaYo listened intently as his brother poured his soul out about the deadly lifestyle he was on the streets living. He knew Quavon was out there grinding, but in all reality, Quavon was out there on some boss shit.

"Quavon, listen, bro, I don't need you up here in the cell next to me. Mama and the rest of the family need you. You are the glue that holds our family together. Do you understand? Quavon, it's only two ways out of this game, that's the penitentiary or the grave. Ain't no happy endings in the dope game."

"Bro it's too late for all that *Malcolm X* shit. Niggas out here got money on my head and I ain't ducking no rec. The same way you wasn't ducking no rec when you was out there," Quavon retorted standing on his manhood.

"All I'm saying bro is that don't mean nothing when you here with a life sentence in one of these U.S.P.s walking the yard for the rest of your life. This shit ain't copped up to what it's supposed to be. Niggas is dying in here.

"Man, listen Yaton, I ain't come here for all that. I just wanted to come up here, hug you, let you know that I love you and let you know what's going on in them streets. The torch you passed me just know I'm carrying that motherfucker whether it's to the pen or the grave, and don't worry about that maggot T.B., I'm a handle that, swiftly." Quavon stood up putting on his jacket.

"Quavon, hold up." YaYo stood. "Listen it's a strong possibility that I might be getting out of here. It's not for certain but I'm fighting—I'm fighting for my life. You just make sure you're out there when I touchdown, and keep that on the low," YaYo said staring his brother in his eyes.

"Bro on my word, I'ma be there. When you touch down I'ma have the G.B.C. red carpet rolled out." Quavon hugged his brother and left the visiting room.

YaYo stood watching his brother exit. He knew Quavon wasn't the same innocent Quavon he remembered. The streets had called and Quavon answered. As he looked into Quavon's eyes it was like looking into the Devil's. YaYo knew Quavon was too far gone. The vicious streets of Chicago had given birth to another savage named, *Quavon*.

CHAPTER 16

Top Cat sat in the back of his Cadillac Escalade, Quavon sat beside him. Benny the driver pulled into the Dan Ryan Expressway headed to downtown Chicago. Top Cat had summoned Quavon to discuss some serious Nation Bizness.

"Quavon, my son, I must say that the structure and finesse you have brung has improved this business remarkably," Top-Cat said lighting his Cuban cigar. Since bringing Quavon into his organization the drug blocks had picked up on the numbers with fewer problems from the soldiers and Quavon and his strategic thinking was the cause of the success.

"It's nothing, big homie. You shine I shine," Quavon replied checking his Facebook.

"You know Quavon words cannot explain the gratitude I have towards you. But our Nation has come across some troubles that could be hazardous to the growth of our operation,

"Oh yeah?" Quavon asked suspiciously looking up from his phone, at Top Cat.

"Yes, I have a mission for you Quavon. There's a Jamaican by the name of Luscious, who's been owing me some paper for a while now."

"How much?" Quavon asked.

"How much does not matter. In the game, you will learn that it's all about principle. Do you understand?" Top Cat schooled blowing the sweet smoke from the Cuban through his nostrils.

"What do you need me to do?"

"I need you to cause his departure from this life. A statement must be made. That is to never bite the hand that feeds you. Now understand you have to be careful when dealing with Luscious, he moves with a lot of men and is always on point. He also has a substantial amount of bodies under his belt. So, be strategic."

Quavon nodded his head in understanding. He knew he had to complete the mission if he wanted a chance to get deeper into Top Cat's circle.

"Don't even trip, Top Cat, I will get right on it. This *small* problem will be taken care of," Quavon said.

"That's what I like to hear." Top Cat slid Quavon a yellow manila envelope. "Inside that folder is the information you will need to assist you in handling this man."

Quavon opened the envelope and stared at the black and white photo of the Jamaican with the long dreads. The man seemed to have a look of cockiness and content. Only if he knew that his treachery was going to lead him to his gravely demise. Quavon put the picture back in the envelope. He wasn't about killing for another individual but he knew it was all part of his plan. He had a bigger picture in mind.

"When you want this clown hit?" Quavon put the envelope in his coat.

"I want this handled asap, the man is stifling my money and what I'm trying to achieve." Top Cat took a pull from the Cigar.

"Say no more, just watch the W.G.N news, I got this."

****

T.B. walked the showroom floor at Prestige Imports in Miami, Florida. Since his Heroin plug used the shipments, the money had been coming in non-stop so T.B. figured he would treat himself to something   foreign.

"Check out the Bentley Bentayga," Band-aid, T.B.'s henchmen said, admiring the new Bentley truck that had just come out.

"Yeah, I peeped it. They want too much for it though. For hundred racks it don't look like shit to me," T.B. replied as he had his eyes set on the lime green *Lamborghini Huracan*. "But this is what I'm talking about." T.B. walked over to the lamb running his hand across the hood of the vehicle.

"Excuse me can I help you gentleman?" A curvy blonde bombshell walked toward the men. She was 5'1' with a phat ass and thick, shapely thighs.

"I was wondering what's the tag on this Lambo?" T.B. asked licking his lips seductively as she began to give him the history on the Lamborghini.

"This here is the Lamborghini Huracan is a 2015 model. It's had one owner and it has 1,500 original miles. This beauty is priced at 276,000. A small price to pay for a car with so much power. Don't you think?" The blonde said with a seductive look of her own.

T.B. felt his meat swell inside his Mauri linen shorts as he mentally envisioned fucking her from the back. The blonde must've noticed the imprint in his shorts because she was immediately turned on by the baller who stood before her as her pussy lips got moist.

"That's it?" T.B. asked and stepped closer to her, her perfume invaded his space. 276,000 wasn't nothing to pay for his new toy.

"How will you be paying for the purchase, sir?" The sexy saleswoman asked, she almost came from the clear diamonds hanging on T.B.'s neck. She had been living in Miami for five years now. Coming from a small town in Nebraska and become accustomed to dating men with lots of drug money and T.B. reeked of it.

"I got two-hundred eighty grand for you ma. Two hundred seventy-six gees for the car and four gees for you to fix the paperwork for me."

The blonde whose name was Kelly had anticipated this and was ready to handle business, this was how she made her money. She agreed and took T.B. into her office to do the paperwork. Once inside the office Kelly closed the door, after locking the door she dropped to her knees. T.B. couldn't believe his luck. Kelly tugged at his Gucci belt and unbuttoned his shorts, freeing his ten-inch monster. Kelly tried her hardest to take all of him in the warmth of her mouth.

"Ahhhhh shit," T.B. moaned while Kelly tried to deepthroat him. Her attempts were futile, and she started to gag. T.B. grabbed a fist full of her long blonde hair and pumped in and out of Kelly's mouth causing tears to fall from her eyes. "Damn, bitch your mouth feels good as shit," T.B. said then felt his volcano about to erupt.

Kelly must've felt it too because she started slurping and jerking his snake faster. T.B. exploded hot nut inside of Kelly's mouth, while she swallowed every drop like it was a vanilla-flavored dessert. She wiped the excess semen from the corner of her mouth with the back of her hand, stood up, and straightened her dress. "Now we can get this paperwork done, Mr."

T.B. just smiled as he pulled up his shorts. Forty-five minutes later, T.B. pulled out of Prestige Imports and was now gliding his new machine down South Beach. *Young Jeezy* poured through the Bose speakers inside the whip. T.B. rapped along with Jeezy as he admired all the beautiful women walking on the sidewalk. He was getting 200 kilos of uncut dope a month. T.B. had his weight up, he was getting bricks of the China White for 30 racks, meaning $30,000 and charging niggas up to $100,000. Not to mention, his breakdown was impeccable. T.B. had blocks and trap spots that were doing no less than 100 gees a day, life was good. The only problem he had was with Quavon. Quavon had signed his own death warrant when he pulled his strap and didn't bust, in a New York minute he would meet his fate. T.B. figured with the money and power he was getting when the shit popped off, he would be ready.

Bandaid sat in the passenger seat of the Lambo checking his Facebook page.

"Oh shit, Bruh that nigga Meek Mill coming to the stadium in two weeks. Everybody on the book talking about that shit!"

"Oh yeah? T.B. said half interested as he slid the Lambo through the streets of Miami.

"You already know the whole city gon' be up in there. We gotta slide through in the Lambo," Bandaid said excitedly.

T.B. thought about it for a minute, what was the sense of having a whip that cost a quarter-mill if you didn't stunt in it. Plus, he wanted to show G.B.C his new toy.

"You already know we gon' pull up in that bitch!" T.B. replied but right now he had his mind set on going to meet the plug to turn in the 200 bands.

He had a few days to kick it in Miami before returning to the Chi and he wanted to enjoy the scene. Plus, he wanted to taste Kelly's fat muffins before he left. Just the thought of ramming his dick in her caused him to swell up. Life was good and he was all the way up. In a minute his name would ring bell's throughout states as one of the most feared drug bosses to play the game.

****

Quavon sat in a low-key minivan parked down the street from a Popeye's chicken on the city's Northside. Roccett occupied the passenger seat with a Draco Ak-47laid across his lap. It had been a week since Top Cat gave him the mission to murder Luscious. Top Cat told Quavon that Luscious had to be dealt with in a strategic manner. After doing surveillance on the Jamaican, Quavon knew that Top Cat had given Luscious too much credit. To Quavon Luscious moved reckless and was somewhat a clown. His movements through the streets were routine. His routine consisted of riding around picking up money from different spots on the Northside. He was always accompanied by the same individuals, three dudes who looked to still be in high school.

Quavon knew that the youngstas had guns with the skinny jeans they rocked, he could see the information on their state I.D. Quavon couldn't seem to figure out the skinny jean error. He looked at the face of his G-Shock watch, the time read 9:15 p.m. for the past week Luscious and his cronies would pull up in the Popeyes parking lot and go into the restaurant to eat, tonight was no different. Quavon looked into his rear-view mirror and saw Luscious' dark green Cadillac DTS pull into the restaurant parking lot. He reached under the driver's seat to retrieved the Glock .357.

Quavon said, "Let's handle this function."

Roccett pulled the slide back on the Draco chambering a round into the chamber. Quavon pulled his black ski-mask over his face and pulled his hoodie over his head. Roccett did the same. Equipped to lay their murder game down they exited the whip and headed for the restaurant.

"Let me get a six-piece, spicy, breasts, fries—four biscuits and a large Sprite, man," Luscious ordered his food.

It had been a long day in the streets, it was starting to get harder and harder to do business. Due to the fact that a lot of his clientele was starting to back away from him because they knew that Top Cat was at his neck and dudes wanted no part in that whatsoever. Luscious had met Top Cat in Vienna State Prison, Top Cat promised Luscious a spot on his organization and an opportunity to make some real money. Little did Top-Cat know Luscious had a serious gambling vice and unfortunately Luscious tricked off 100 gees of Top Cats' money. Instead of trying to hustle up Top Cat's bread he chose to say fuck 'em and go on the run. Now he was hiding out and getting money on the North Side.

"So, will that be for here or to go?" the cashier asked.

"For here, Mon," Luscious replied in his strong Jamaican accent.

"Your total comes to thirty-two dollars and fifteen cents." Luscious pulled out a big wad of money, peeled off two twenties and paid for his food.

After getting his change they sat at the table by the window. The sour-diesel Kush they'd just smoked had them hungry as shit, so they dove into their meals like it would be their last. Luscious was on his third piece of Chicken when two masked men entered the establishment both pointing firearms. One of the men announced a robbery and demanded the cashier to open the cash register. The cashier did as he was told, handing the robber the small bills. Luscious looked over at his goons who were both visibly shaken, as well Luscious. One of the men walked over to their table and pointed his weapon.

"Come up off the chain!" The robber sneered from behind the mask.

"Okay, man," Luscious replied taking the chain from around his neck.

One of his goons tried to make a play for the .45 that was concealed on his waist until a loud '*Booom*' rang out in the small restaurant. The young goon's head exploded from the 357 slug that split his shit to the white meat, warm crimson red blood and brain tissue splattered Luscious' face. It was a do or die situation. Luscious reached of his gun, his attempt was exempt as Roccett pulled the trigger on the Draco.

Cha! Cha! Cha! Cha! Cha! The baby choppa spit venom hitting Luscious in his chest and face and his goon in the throat. Pandemonium broke out in the restaurant, Luscious was slumped over on the table in a puddle of his own blood but yet still breathing until Quavon shot him in the back of the head silencing him for eternity.

Quavon and Roccett ran out of the restaurant and into the cold streets of the Chi.

"This is Vanessa Jenson and Tom Walbert, you're tuned into WGN News at nine. On today's top story two gunmen walked into a Popeyes Chicken on Howard and Damen on the city's Northside. Witnesses say the two men walked in with guns and pronounced a robbery. After robbing the cashier the men shot and killed three men in cold blood. Police have released the names of the deceased, forty-year-old Luscious Macmella, eighteen-year-old Danni Simms and twenty-year-old Russell Green. These homicides have been added to the already high extensive murder rate totaling seven hundred and fifty murders just this year. Police would like anyone with information on the men who caused this horrific crime to please contact local law enforcement."

Top Cat smiled as he took a sip from his Hennessy, turning off the news, his lovely wife, Bella sat on his lap. Seeing Luscious's face on the news let him know he'd made the right choice bringing Quavon into his organization, in due time he would be able to expand his operation.

"Why you smiling so hard?" his wife asked putting her arms around his neck.

"We're going to the top, baby. We're going to the top!"

S. Allen

CHAPTER 17

It was Saturday and YaYo was in his cell reading a *Don-Diva* magazine, his celly Paco was on the top bunk passed out. YaYo was waiting for the count to be cleared so he could hit the yard. He had a lot on his mind mainly his case. Mr. B had told him he had a strong possibility of overturning the life sentence, and ever since then, that had been his primary focus. He had to get out of prison and back out there with his family. He still hadn't heard from Shakira and he hadn't even attempted to call her. The news Quavon put in his lap during the visit had crushed him. He loved Shakira and knew one day, she would move on. He didn't expect her to wait her whole life for him, but never in a million years did he think she would fuck his right-hand man. The more thoughts of T.B. sexing his wife caused his chest to tighten up.

All he and T.B. had been through in the game meant nothing. He would've laid in the ground for T.B. and the G.B.C, it was living proof when he stood in front of the government and was handed the life sentence—never folding.

YaYo remembered Rivera's words when he was in Cook County Jail, "Neva love the game, YaYo because it will never love you back."

YaYo's thoughts were interrupted when his cell was unlocked, he looked out and was shocked to see C.O. Sanchez standing at the door.

"Anderson, I need you to come down and empty all the trash, then place them in the hallway please?"

YaYo was the head orderly on the unit and his job was to keep the unit clean. All for a measly $10.00 a month. YaYo looked at her suspiciously seeing that the afternoon count would be cleared in thirty minutes, but he slipped on his shoes and walked out of the cell. C.O. Sanchez locked the cell back and followed YaYo down the steps.

After retrieving all the trash bags on the unit totaling six in all, YaYo placed the bags by the door that led to the back hallway. Office Sanchez was on the phone in the officer's station when YaYo walked up. Her hair was slicked back in a neat ponytail and her *Mac* lip gloss made her look delicious, not to mention her *Burberry* perfume had the office smelling fruity.

YaYo stared at her for a minute. She looked so damn exotic to him. Her caramel complexion had a shine to it like her skin had been softly kissed by the sun. Her slanted eyes added to get uniqueness.

Officer Sanchez gave YaYo a provocative look before she ended her call. "Can I help you, Mr. Anderson?" she said standing up from behind the desk.

YaYo eyed her thick thighs and big titties, ever since his visit he'd daydreamed about fucking C.O. Sanchez. "I was just letting you know I grabbed all the trash. You can take me back to my cell."

C.O Sanchez walked from behind the desk. "I need you to take them to the first floor in the hallway," she said and led the way to the back door.

YaYo took notice of how fat her ass was, the tight uniform had her voluptuous ass cheeks fitting snug. After using her key to open the door, she stepped to the side to let YaYo enter the hallway. Once he grabbed some bags and stepped into the hallway, YaYo heard the door close behind him before he was roughly pushed up against the wall. Next thing he knew C.O. Sanchez's tongue was in his mouth. YaYo could taste the double-mint gum on her tongue as he forcefully kissed her back. He dropped the bags on the floor, then caressed her soft ass. His dick was harder than Chinese Arithmetic, threatening to bust from the confines of his Khakis.

"Give it to me, Mr. Anderson. We only got fifteen minutes before they clear the count," C.O. Sanchez said unbuckling her belt.

She didn't have to tell YaYo twice, his pants were down to his ankles in a New York minute. YaYo almost bust a nut at the sight of C.O. Sanchez's thick caramel thighs, her pussy was so fat and wet you could see the wetness through her thong. She put her hands on the rail of the stairs and bent over giving YaYo a front-row seat to their love box. Without a minute to waste, he pulled her to the side and slid his dick inside of her hot juicy walls. She fit him like a glove as she tightened her pussy muscles around his thick, wide meat. C.O. Sanchez had to bite down on her bottom lip to keep her from screaming in pleasure. YaYo was filling her to capacity as he pumped in and out of her. Her ass cheeks jiggled with each thrust, her pussy juices leaked down the inside of her thick thighs making a puddle on the floor.

"Oh my God, Yaton, I'm about to cum! Oh shit, I'm coming, baby!"

"Damn, this pussy so good." YaYo squeezed her ass cheeks harder, she could feel every inch of him as well as the veins in his dick. Then it happened, YaYo exploded his hot nut into her. "Damn girl," was all he could say as he pulled his semi-erect dick from her love box.

C.O. Sanchez swore she saw white dots when she climaxed. "Damn, boy, I see you got that magic stick." She giggled, then kissed him on his lips while he pulled up his pants. They had exactly five minutes before the count was cleared.

Officer Sanchez walked YaYo back to his cell and gave him a wink. He returned the jester, YaYo couldn't believe he'd just banged badass Ms. Sanchez, but little did he know their newfound relationship was about to be an exciting long journey.

****

"So, what you're trying to tell me is that we are not going to be getting the regular tobacco anymore? We gon' be getting the real deal?" YaYo asked Huey while they worked laps on B-Yard.

"Yep, mi friend, *Newports, Camels, Marlboros, and Kools.* And guess what, they are all going to be longs."

YaYo rubbed his freshly trimmed goatee trying to do the math on the hustle. "So, what can I make off one cigarette?" YaYo asked.

"My friend you can break each one down to six-packs, it's twenty cigarettes in a pack so that's like one-hundred eighty books. Almost six-hundred dollars off a pack easy!"

YaYo thought about it for a quick minute, it was definitely a good flip depending on how much Huey would give him the packs for. "So, how much you gonna charge me?"

Huey let out a small chuckle before he answered the question. "YaYo, I fuck with you and I also know that you hustle for a cause. We never have any money issues. So, this what I'ma do for you, my friend. I'll give you the packs for forty-five books. So, one-fifty, whatever you buy I will front you on consignment. You feel me?" YaYo thought about how much he had in the stash.

"What you do for a thousand books, amigo?" YaYo said with a smile. The greed could be seen all on Huey's fat round face.

"For a thousand books my friend, your boy Huey gon' bless your game and real nice. For that, I'ma give you two cartons and front you two. Think you can handle that?"

YaYo looked at him like he was crazy. "Say no more, migo."

"I guess I will see you on the next move?" Huey said shaking YaYo's hand.

YaYo saw the dollar signs that danced in his mind and thoughts. You can take a nigga out the game but you can't take the hustle out the nigga. YaYo walked in Mr. B's cell and peeked in to see Mr. B at his small desk, bombarded in paperwork. YaYo knocked respectfully before Mr. B waved him to enter the cell.

"What's up, Mr. B? Sorry to bother you I was just checking in on you old-head," YaYo said and took a seat in a chair.

Mr. B mugged YaYo. "Watch that old-head shit. Only thing old about me is my bankroll. I might be old in age, but I can still run with you youngstas." Mr. B took off his glasses and place them on the table.

YaYo knew Mr. B was a savage in the work out department, when he wasn't doing law work, he was pushing up the concrete doing a million burpees. Mr. B was the truth.

"Anyhow I'm glad you stopped by, I wanted to speak with you about your case. In order for me to help you, you have to give me the truth in this matter."

"Like I said Mr. B and like it says in my paperwork they were extorting me. I was kicking in almost twenty grand a month"

"And then what?" Mr. B asked.

"They figured I was starting to get more money, so they tried to up the fee to two-hundred grand a month. Fifty gees a week."

"And I take it you didn't accept the fee?"

"Fuck naw, I told them to go to hell. Then they threatened me about turning in some tape from a C.I. who said I confessed to him about a murder when I was in juvenile prison."

"I see—I see. Did they play the taped confession at your trail? Because I don't see it in the trial transcripts," Mr. B said.

"No, they didn't."

"Did the rat who was confessed on the stand at your trial know?"

"Nope."

"Why not?"

"The nigga somehow disappeared and they couldn't locate him." Mr. B shook his head in disgust, he hated how the government railroaded so many black men who was ignorant to the system and ended up getting buried in Prison cemeteries, "Now this cop that was indicted on your case. Where is he?"

"Last I heard they were shipping him to U.S.P. Victorville in California," YaYo replied.

Mr. B clasped his hands in front of his face as if he was in heavy thought. "We have to find a way to get to him. If we can get him in court with us and get him to recant his statement. Say that he falsified evidence and he started the bogus investigation on you. It would help us greatly."

"Why would he do that, Mr. B?" YaYo had a confused look on his face.

"Because maybe he wants to stay alive. Now I'm going to file a motion called a 2255 and see where that takes us. A lot of witnesses on your case are either missing or are not credible witnesses that can be found. All I need you to do is stay out of trouble and let me work my magic. Deal?"

"Mr. B you already know, I'm definitely trying to get back to them streets. 50 Cent said, I got a lot of living to do before I die, and I ain't got time to waste."

Later on that night, YaYo was in his cell with a razor blade, bogies, and enough cigarettes to give the entire B.O.P. cancer. He had received his pack from Huey and now it was time to get to the money. Pook stood outside the cell on security to make sure the C.O. didn't walk up on YaYo while he was in the cell handling his business.

"Aye YaYo what's good with Mr. B and your case? You ain't really been chatting it up with me about it?" Paco probed from the top bunk.

"For real bruh, I just don't want to get too excited, then shit don't happen like I want them to. I'ma be sick, feel me? It's plenty of niggas in here that's been sold dreams but, yet, they're still here doing time. I just ain't trying to be one of those niggas," YaYo said slicing a piece off a Newport long and tying it in a plastic bag.

"Yeah, I know fam but you know the saying—different strokes for different folks."

"I feel that too. To keep it 'G' from what Mr. B saying I got a seventy-five percent chance of bouncing up outta this graveyard."

"That's what's up. Just make it count when you get outta here. Don't go out there chasing behind motherfuckas that ain't send you nothing," Paco said quoting a line from one of Plies songs.

"You already know, bruh, nothing but family."

It took YaYo an hour and a half to bag up all the cigarettes. Now he was ready to get on his friend. Things were starting to look up. He had a chance of getting free. He was getting money and had a badass C.O. bitch on his dick. In his mind, he was still—that nigga.

****

"Shamira bring your lil' ass here so I can put your clothes on!" Shakira yelled at her daughter aggravated as hell.

Her stress level was to its peak. YaYo had blocked her from his email and she had written him several times in the last month but he hadn't even attempted to write he back. YaYo had completely cut her off, no more phone calls, emails—nothing. She knew Quavon had spilled the beans on the situation with her and T.B. but how could she blame him. She knew she was dead wrong and had crossed the line in the first place, but at the time she was weak and vulnerable, and T.B. took advantage of her. She knew she had to get back in good graces with her baby daddy, if not for her, but on the strength of their daughter. After getting Shamira dressed for day-care, Shakira got her phone, called O'Hare Airport and booked a flight to Louisiana. Whether YaYo wanted to hear from her and his daughter or not, they were on their way.

****

Karen noticed Quavon's car parked in the driveway when she came home. She got out of her car and went inside the house in search of him. She didn't find him upstairs, so she went to the base-ment door. "Quavon, you down there?" she yelled down into the basement. Receiving no response, Karen flicked on the light switch and proceed down the stairs where she found him sprawled out on the sectional. "Quavon, didn't you hear me calling you?"

Before he could respond, she noticed an empty bottle of Ciroc sitting on the glass sofa table next to a large band of money and a gun with a long-extended clip attached to it.

Karen's brows knitted and her mouth morphed into a straight, angry line. She walked over to Quavon and popped him upside the head.

"Ma! What's wrong with you?" he said.

"Boy, why you got a damn gun in my house? And where did you get all that money?" she bellowed.

Quavon sat up, grabbed the Glock 19 and put it on his waist without even attempting to explain. He had been going through a lot the past few days. Every time he fell asleep he would have vi-sions of the people he killed. Since YaYo had been in the FEDs, Quavon had caught four bodies. He wondered if YaYo had dreams and nightmares about the people he had killed. Either way, Quavon had no regrets. He knew that before it was all said and done, he would add more bodies to his list.

His mother's fussing brought him out of his reverie. "You listen to me, Quavon, and you listen good! I don't know exactly what you're in them streets doing, or what you're involved in. Whatever it is, I don't want the ghetto shit around me or my family. You're going down the same path Yaton chose, and you see what that got him -- life in prison." A tear ran down Karen's face as she continued, "You dropped out of school just to run the streets. You don't listen to me anymore, and you wanna be grown! Well, go ahead, but I'm not gonna stand by and wait for the consequences. Get your shit and get your black ass outta my house. And don't come back until you've got your shit together!" Karen screamed.

Quavon stood up and pulled his Gucci hoodie over his head. He grabbed his keys off the table and attempted to speak. "Ma, I—"

"I don't want to hear it, Quavon! Get out!"

It truly hurt Karen to put her son out, but her hands were tied. He was a grown-ass man, playing grown man games, but she would not let him do that in her house.

"Okay, Ma." Quavon made his way to the stairs before something hit him in the back.

"And take that shit with you!" his mother spat.

Quavon turned around and saw the wad of money at his feet. It was ten grand. "But I want you to have it," he pleaded.

"I don't need that shit, I work for mines!" she yelled.

Quavon took to the steps leaving the money where it laid and leaving his mother in tears.

CHAPTER 18

Quavon pulled into the parking lot of Apple Bees on the far Southside. He had called a meeting with his staff to discuss some Nation bizness. It was time to get the wheels in motion on the first part of his plan. Shit was about to get real—real quick. At the thought of his financial success Crusha's SL 550 Benz pulled behind his BMW, Reggie 'G' occupied the passenger seat as Choppa sat in the back. Quavon stepped out of his whip and hit the remote locking the doors.

The guys stepped out of the Benz to greet Quavon.

"What's good, Killa?" Crusha said pulling the hood of his mink coat over his head to shield him from the icy wind.

"Ain't shit waiting on y'all so we can get to this business," Quavon replied.

"Well, let's get to it," Reggie 'G' said as the men entered the restaurant.

Once seated in a booth in the back of the establishment the gangsters ordered double shots of 1800 Tequila.

When the waitress returned with their drinks, she asked, "Are you gentlemen ready to order?"

"Not yet, lil' mama, give us a few more minutes, please," replied Choppa.

"No problem. Take your time. Just let me know when you are ready. I'll be back." The redbone sashayed off, putting a little more switch in her hips.

Quavon took the stage and raised his shot glass. "I want to make a toast." The others raised their glasses as Quavon continued, "I want to make a toast to us, the real G.B.C. A toast to love, life and the loyalty our organization was built on. I also want to make a toast to our fallen soldiers who lived and died by the Creed that we continue to live by R.I.P. Last but not least I want to toast to our Chief who has paved the way for us in these streets to be a force to be reckoned with. Free YaYo!"

"Free YaYo!" the men said clicking their glasses together solidifying their brotherhood.

After downing their shots Quavon got right to business. "Check this out, my niggas, this the business. Like I told y'all before, this old nigga Top Cat is getting that money on the Westside. It's time to start shuffling that shit down. Now this dummy made a grave mistake of appointing me as his Chief of Security. I know all the traps and the stash houses." Crusha smiled. "I know what time his blocks open and what time they close."

"Damn, how you know all that?" Choppa asked.

Quavon looked at him with an expression that said, '*What kind of dumb ass question is that.*' "Because I'm in charge of that," Quavon said answering the question. "Now like I was saying I know the ends and outs to this nigga's infrastructure. Now it's time to exploit it."

"What's on your mind youngsta?" Reggie 'G' asked, liking where this was going.

"My niggas this the play. We gon' rob all the traps and stash houses strategically. The only way you can hurt a man is by hurting his pockets," Quavon schooled remembering the game his brother taught him many years back. "And at the same time, we gon' use Top Cat's soldiers to hit up T.B.'s spots on the Southside." Everybody remained silent.

Crusha immediately saw Quavon in a new light. Not only was he a hustla, but a master of deceit, looking at Quavon was like seeing YaYo in the flesh.

"We gon' take everything from that nigga T.B. including his life," Quavon said as his eyes turned a shade red giving him an evil appearance.

"What about the old nigga out West?" Crusha asked.

"When it's all said and done, I'ma punish him personally. And when the smoke clears we gon' have the city on lock and key. Our dope or no dope gets sold in the city. Niggas gon' either get down or lay down."

"So, where we fit in at?" Crusha said loving the diabolical plan being laid out.

"Crusha, you the money man. So, I'm a need you to collect and hold our funds we about to snatch from these fake niggas. I'm trusting you my dude so don't let me down."

"Don't even trip I got this, Quavon."

"Reggie, I need you to find us a steady connect while we in the midst of the bullshit. Cause once it's said and done, we gon' need our work on the streets to be consistent. Feel me?"

"Roger that family, I think I got somebody in mind. A cat out in Calumet City but we gotta be grabbing a hundred keys or better before he even thinks about serving us."

"Get on his line, we coming for them birds.

"What about me, Quavon?" Choppa said feeling left out.

"Choppa this what I need you to do." Quavon passed him a piece of paper with an address written on it.

"My nigga you the sword. You ready to get your feet wet?"

"Come on fam you already know. That's what I do," Choppa said ready to kill somebody.

"Now it's gon' be plenty heat out here with the police concerning the bodies that's gonna start dropping, but the beauty of it all is they ain't gon' know who hitting who. That's the sweet part."

"What about T.B. and them?" Crusha asked.

"Y'all worry about Top Cat and his cronies. I got them, niggas, out South. It's a new day my niggas, we about to eat and those that's not eating with us gon' starve. The plans had been set in stone, now the only thing left to do is execute them. The streets of Chicago is about to produce a violent film and all are welcomed with front row seats to the murda show."

Later that night Quavon slid through the grit and grime of Chicago's Westside. He pulled up at a stoplight on Kedzie and Vanburen, grabbed his iPhone and dialed Roccett's number.

The phone rang three times before Roccett's raspy voice came over the receiver. "What's good, shawty?" Roccett spoke.

"What's up, my nigga? Look I'm on your side of town meet me on Augusta down Springfield at JJ's fish in ten minutes."

"Say no more," was Roccett's only reply before he disconnected the call.

The light turned green and Quavon slid across the intersection en-route to meet up with Roccett until something caught his attention on the radio. He turned it up, it was a commercial promoting a *Meek Mill* concert at the United Center. Quavon fucked with Meek hard and couldn't believe Meek Mill as coming to do a show in the Motherland.

'*Damn, a nigga gotta catch that, all the hoes gon' be out,*' he thought to himself.

He had been in the streets hard so he figured he would take a day off and kick it. He hadn't seen Davon in a minute and the Meek Mill concert would be right up his twin's alley. Davon was due to graduate from college next semester for graphic design. He and Davon were supposed to walk across the stage together but the wicked streets had consumed his life and everything in it.

Quavon felt he'd let his family down and it hurt his soul. But there was no turning back, he had to finish what he'd started. He was going to get up with his brother and show him the time of his life. Ten minutes later, Quavon pulled into the parking lot of JJ's fish. Roccett sat in his beat-up Chevy Caprice that had seen better days. He took another pull of his Black & Mild cigar before he got out of his car and slid in the passenger seat of Quavon's BMW X5.

"What's good fam?"

"Same ole shit, staying low trying to get to the doe," Roccett replied.

Quavon put the whip in drive and pulled out of the parking lot. "Check this fam. Your uncle paying you a nice lil' penny to handle his functions, right?" Quavon glanced at Roccett through his peripheral vision.

Yeah. Why what's up?"

"Listen, my nigga, I'm a get right to the point. I see you a real nigga and your ambition is high as hell. It's time for you to position yourself as a boss. The time is changing Roccett and niggas like us gotta change with them feel me?" Rocett nodded his head in understanding. "I'm trying to put you in a position to be that nigga."

"How you gon' do that?" Roccett asked trying to see where this was going.

"Roccett, have you ever heard of the G.B.C?"

"Who hasn't heard of the G.B.C?"

"Like I said time is changing and if niggas don't change with them they gon' be lost in the sauce and become food for niggas like us." Quavon definitely had Roccett's undivided attention. "What would you say if I told you I knew where all the stash houses and trap spots owned by the G.B.C. are and that it was sweet?"

"I'd say put a nigga down," Roccett replied with greed dripping off his tone. "But what's the catch, shawty?"

"The catch is—everybody in them has to die." Quavon was now looking Roccett in his eyes.

"I'm in," was Roccett's only reply.

Quavon and Roccett rode around the city chopping it up and burning gas as Quavon gave Roccett all the information he needed to assist him in dismantling T.B. and his bogus operation.

Click! Clack! was the sound of the slide chambering a 223 Caliber Winchester round into the deadly chamber of Choppa's Bushmaster assault rifle. The 100-round clip was filled to capacity. Choppa looked at the paper Quavon had given him once more to make sure the address was correct. He looked at the building seeing the number 1048 and knew he was at the right address. The slow traffic of fiends coming to the building confirmed it. He slid the compact rifle into a large Domino's Pizza box and pulled the Domino's Pizza hat over his short dreadlocks to match the uniform. He looked in the rearview mirror, satisfied with his appearance, then stepped out of the vehicle. It was time to put on for his click.

****

"That's right bitch, suck this big dick," Dime-Bag moaned as a thick, dark-skinned chick tried her best to deepthroat his nine inches of meat.

Dime bag was on the clock overseeing the trap spot waiting for Quavon to come and relieve him of his duties. Dime-Bag didn't care too much for Quavon one bit. He had witnessed first-hand when Quavon came into Top Cat's organization and secured the chief of security   spot.

A position he had been trying to obtain since he'd joined Top Cat's gang when he was only thirteen years old. To see Quavon handed the position on a silver platter made him sick to his stomach. In his wicked mind, he thought would catch Quavon slipping and when he did, he would lay him down. Until then he would just play his position as a foot-soldier.

Feeling his climax Dime-Bag grabbed a hand full of the girl's weave and began pumping her face even faster. The tip of his tool hit her tonsils making her gag. "Ahhhh shit." He released his seed impregnating her esophagus.

The chick continued to suck on his semi-erect dick until he was satisfied and she'd drained his nut-sac. Satisfied with her work she gave the tip of his dick one last suck causing a popping noise like her lips were a suction cup. After finishing his sexual escapade Dime-Bag put on his Prada jogging pants, laced up his black ACG Nike boots and got back focused in grind mode.

"Where the hell is the clown ass nigga, Quavon? Got a nigga on his time and shit," Dime-Bag sneered.

Everything Quavon did irritated him. Bolo was about to respond to Dime-Bag's question when there was a knock at the front door.

"That's probably his bitch ass right there," Dime-Bag mumbled under his breath.

Bolo went to the door and looked out the peephole. Seeing the man in uniform holding a pizza box reminded him that he hadn't eaten all day, his stomach pains faulted his mind state and caused him to make a deadly mistake

"Pizza Man!" Bolo said over his bark all the while unlocking the front door.

He opened the door seeing the pizza man's smile was the last thing Bolo saw and then a flash. After that complete darkness as he was shot point-blank range in the face. The 223 ammunition gave the rifle a minor recoil as the back from the chopper broke the silence in the night.

Seeing his potna's brains explode and his body drop made Dime-Bag get active and pull his Glock. *Boc! Boc! Boc! Boc!* Dime-Bag squeezed on the trigger in an attempt to save his life from the home invader that was trying to kill him. The workers at the table began screaming from the violent scene being displayed before them.

Cha! Cha! Cha! Cha! Cha! was the response of Choppa's rifle damaging anything that the slugs hit.

"Nigga you ain't about this Murda shit—you faking!" Choppa growled antagonizing his enemy. Advancing inside the trap spot with murder on his mind Choppa was determined to finish the mission, stepping over the body he'd just dropped. Choppa aimed his gun at the naked workers in the kitchen and applied pressure to the trigger mechanism, spraying them down with hollow-point led. The house reeked of death and gun smoke.

Boc! Boc! Boc! Dime-Bag's Glock spit as he fired from behind a couch almost hitting Choppa with the 9mm. Choppa held onto the trigger swinging the full auto 223 in Dime-Bag's direction cutting the couch in half. Hot shell cases fell to the carpet as Choppa emptied the magazine, slugs cut through the couch like butter with Dime-Bag catching twelve of them, six in the upper torso and six in the facial and head area. After securing the premises making sure nobody was alive, Choppa wiped his fingerprints from the murder weapon with his T-Shirt and left it in the bloody living room then made his exit.

A lot had forgotten about his side of the game, blinded by the money and drugs. You had hustlers and you had killlas. It was war and if nigga's murder game wasn't proper, niggas wasn't going to be able to see Quavon and the real G.B.C.

S. Allen

CHAPTER 19

It was 10:15 p.m. when Quavon pulled his new S Class Benz into the parking lot of the United center on the city's Westside. The crowd was thick, and it seemed as if all the ballers in the city came out to show *Meek Mill* some Chi-Town love. Foreign whips graced the parking lot, Beamers, Benzes, and Trucks were just a few in the sea of exotic cars.

"There go a spot, right there," Davon said from the passenger side. This was his first time going to a concert and he was excited, to say the least.

"Man, it's some bad bitches out here! This nigga, Meek done brought all the hoes out!" Reggie 'G' said between pulls of the Sour Diesel he was puffing on.

After Quavon parked the Benz they all got out. Quavon was dressed to impress in all white *Da Vinci*. He rocked an icy pair of *Air Force Ones* to compliment his outfit, his 32-inch platinum chain with the Jesus piece along with his *Cervix Rolex* gave him a grown-up look. Davon chose to keep things simple with a Navy-Blue Jean outfit. Reggie 'G' was dressed down in all army fatigue, dressing the part of the soldier and his dreads hung past his shoulders.

A group of females walked past them as they got out of the car.

"Damn, girl that nigga look like money," one of the chicks said eyeing Quavon.

A confident smirk was visible on Quavon's face. He was the man and he knew it.

As they walked toward the stadium Quavon's attention was on a green Lambo that had just swerved into the parking lot. He'd never seen a Lamborghini up close so the whip had his undivided attention, but what happened next blew his mind. The Lambo pulled up on one side of him and his people coming to a screeching halt before the doors came up. Two Porches Cayennes pulled behind the Lambo. Quavon couldn't believe who stepped out of the vehicle.

"What's good, lil' nigga? The city isn't as big as it seems, huh?" T.B. said stepping out of the Lamborghini. His jewelry shined off his neck, ears, and wrist. The handle of his Glock .40 was visible on the hip of his Balmain Jeans. His goons hopped out of the Porches trucks.

A sneer came across Quavon's mouth, he wanted to crush T.B. right on the spot but he knew it wasn't the time and place.

"I guess it's not so small, I'ma see you around, though. Come on, Davon." Quavon stepped off with his brother.

"You dead out here, shawty. I'ma see you again and on my soul next time I'ma kill your ass, believe that."

Quavon stopped in his tracks and looked back at T.B. who had his hand on his pole.

"Come on fam, later for that fake sucka. We gon' check all that killa shit in one minute," Reggie 'G' said, he couldn't wait till the time came to lay the murder down on T.B.

Quavon let the death threat roll of his shoulders. He had to keep control over his emotions, he was playing chess not checkers. One thing for sure, T.B. would die for his disrespect, that he was sure of.

"Come on family let's go enjoy this concert, fuck that nigga," was Quavon's reply.

Quavon, Davon and Reggie 'G' popped bottles of Ciroc and thugged out to *Meek Mill's Dreams and Nightmares*. "I used to pray four times like this," Quavon rapped with the bottle in the air and his Rolex blingin'. "All the time I spent on some locked up shit." The liquor and weed had him feeling good and seeing his brother having a good time made all his dreams and troubles in the streets seem worth it.

"Damn, I love you, bro!" Quavon said hugging his brother.

"Man, we out here with all these chicks and you wanna hug up on me?" Davon joked.

"Nigga, I don't care about these hoes. You my twin and I love you, nigga!" Quavon took a swig from the bottle.

While Quavon and Davon were at the Meek Mill concert Roccett sat low-key in his Chevy Caprice, a Kevlar vest covered his chest, black Nike gloves on his hands and a shot-gun with a 20-round drum attached to it, a street sweeper. He was parked on a dark street on 137th and Lowe on the Southside of the city. He was watching the row houses on the block and the stash house for the G.B.C.

where money and drugs were kept. Roccett watched as a black Maxima left the house and was hoping like hell that it would return soon. All his hopes and prayers were answered when the Maxima pulled back up in front of the row-house an hour later. Not wasting any time he cocked the 12-gauge and slid out of the Chevy and crept up on his prey. The man that got out of the Maxima never heard or saw it coming, all he felt was the cold steel that was now planted on his exposed neck.

"Put the key in the door and open it nice and slow. You make a move, I'ma blow your motherfucking brains out," Roccett sneered from behind the black ski-mask.

The man began to shake as the threat of death invaded his mind-frame, fumbling with the keys he said, "Man, ain't nothing in here, I'm just—"

"Shut the fuck up and open the door." Roccett pressed the cold steel harder against the man's neck.

After a few nervous attempts the door opened, Roccett forcefully pushed him inside making him fall face first. Two dudes playing a video game on a large flat screen froze like a deer in headlights at the sight of the masked man with a shotgun pointed at them. One of them thought about life or death and was about to reach for the 9 under the couch cushion.

"You reach and I'ma crush your bitch ass, shawty." The man changed his mind with the quickness. "Now get up and lay down next to your potna." The two thugs did as they were told and laid on the floor next to their homie. "I'ma ask y'all niggas one time and one time only. Where the money and drugs?"

"Man, you know who you fucking with? We work for T.B., nigga," one of the men said. The one that was going to reach for the hammer on the couch.

Roccett calmly walked over to him, put the gauge to the back of his head and pulled the trigger. *Booomm!* The deer slug demolished his cranium. Roccett cocked the shotgun ejecting the hot shell to the floor.

"Now let's try this again. Where is the money and drugs?" The smell of fresh death engulfed the crib.

"The money's behind the stove. The work is in the wall behind the T.V.," one of the soldiers confessed.

Roccett pulled out zip ties for his hoodie and secured their wrists and ankles, restricting them from any movement. After pulling the TV off the wall Roccett was shocked to see the hole in the wall, as he reached in the hole he could feel Ziploc freezer bags full of money and began pulling them out. It was six in all, all stuffed with American Currency. A chill ran down his spine at the sight of all the big faces. Next, he went into the kitchen and removed the stove only to see bricks upon bricks of kilos. Making a quick count he counted thirty bricks. After loading a few garbage bags with the money and dope, he picked back up the shotgun.

"Come on bro you got what you came for, let us be," the man lying on the floor pleaded for his life.

Little did he know his pleas for mercy fell on deaf ears. *Booom! Boomm! Booom! Boom!* Roccett gave each man two to the head, sending them into the afterlife leaving the row house with thirty kilos, at least a quarter-million in cash and a triple homicide.

The *Meek Mill* concert was over, Davon, Quavon and Reggie 'G' had balled out for the occasion.

"Bruh, you get ole girl number in the red Donna Karan dress that was in your face all night?" Quavon asked his brother. Davon just started smiling hard as shit. "Let me find out you were at the Meek concert studying for an exam!" Quavon joked.

"Yeah, I got her number. Since you speaking on school you need to get your ass back in school so you can graduate with me," Davon said seriously.

"Like I said bro that school shit ain't for me. That's your lane, not mine."

"Man, you trippin'," Davon said, in regards to his brother's ignorance.

"They say Meek throwing an after-party at the congress downtown, let's pull up down there," Reggie 'G' said from the back seat, he was strolling through his Facebook and just found out the party was not far from over.

"What's up, bro?" You trying to breeze through that joint? See if you can run into shorty in the Red dress," Quavon said pulling up to a red light on Madison Avenue.

"Naw I'm good, I'm tired and I got some studying to do tomorrow.

"Reggie 'G' I told you this nigga was a nerd!" Quavon replied before a black Charger pulled up on the passenger side of the Benz and the back window rolled down.

Boc! Boc! Boc! Boc! Gunshots erupted.

"Oh, shit!" Quavon ducked low and floored the pedal to the Benz.

Boc! Boc! Boc! A gunman held an FNH handgun out of the back window letting it go!

Quavon raced down Madison Avenue while the Charger made a left on Kedzie Street, leaving gun smoke and shell cases.

"Bro I think I'm hit." Reggie 'G' was in the back seat, the 5.62mm round went in and out of his right arm that was now bleeding profusely.

"Davon, help Reggie 'G' back there, I gotta get fam to the hospital," Quavon said with his nerves shook from the shooting. "Davon, you heard what I said?" Quavon glanced at his brother who was leaning against the door with his eyes rolling in the back of his head.

"Davon! Davon!" Quavon tried to shake his brother awake "Fuck!" Quavon started pounding on the steering wheel seeing the blood coming from his brother's mouth only enraged him more. "Davon, wake up bro! Please, Davon!"

Quavon pulled into the emergency room of MT Sini Hospital and jumped out of the whip, paramedics and doctors rushed out of the hospital.

"What happened, sir."

"My brother and my friend just got shot," Quavon replied through a stream of warm tears.

Quavon watched as his twin and one of his loyal soldiers were loaded onto stretchers and raced into the hospital. The gunshots still rang loud in his ears as his brother's blood stained his hands. He had brought his twin out to have a good time and instead put him in the line of fire. He just hoped and prayed that his brother would make it if he didn't his life would be meaningless.

CHAPTER 20

United States Penitentiary Victorville was located in California on the country's West Coast. The prison was a maximum security facility that housed some of America's most high-profile criminals. The majority of the inmates designated to Victorville were violent, had mental problems or just all-out had a boatload of time, and Lloyd Thomas also known as Batman had a combination of all three. After being convicted of tampering with evidence and extortion. The United States Government being that he was law enforcement gave him a three hundred and sixty months sentence which equals a total of thirty years.

Batman never would have thought in a million years he would see Federal Prison. The same federal prison he'd sent countless drug dealers and gang members from the City of Chicago. On the streets, he and his partner Robin worked on the gang and homicide task force. They were to dismantle organized crime and target drug activity throughout the Southside of the city, but deep inside Batman held an evil grudge against gangs and dope pushers. So, did his now deceased partner Robin. Instead of protecting and serving the community of Chicago from the predators, the two detectives chose to extort, rob and kill them, for their own personal gain, thus making them the predators amongst the prey.

Batman and Robin's lives changed when they met YaYo. A smart, unique, criminal-minded street boss that started a ruthless criminal organization, The Get It Boy Click. He felt he could muscle YaYo and the G.B.C out of their street riches but found out they were up against a different kind of beast. One that was willing to take it to the next level. Batman never thought YaYo would hit hard and give the order to have him murdered. He escaped the Grim Reaper, but his partner Robin wasn't so lucky. An AK-47 split his head in half and severed his whole neck almost decapitating him. Batman was shot in the legs and was now used a cane three years later to walk with.

Being shot was something that he could live with, but thirty years in a Federal Pen was not. The whole time the G.B.C. had a confidential informant inside their circle that spilled the beans not only on YaYo's role as an acting gang chief for The Get It Boy Click but also his and Robin's role as extortionist, drug dealers, and murderers. They sold weapons to G.B.C and gave them information on their rivals. Thirty years in Federal Prison was starting to take its toll on Batman. No longer was he the big bad wolf on the streets, now he was a greying old man whose legs hurt every time it rained. Luckily for him, it never really rained in California.

Batman was down bad as far as his financial situation. He had no friends and no family except for the ones he had met in prison, which were very few. Who wanted to be friends with an ex-cop? His first couple of years in Victorville was terrible, he was jumped on countless occasions, robbed and even sexually assaulted. Batman learned the prison politics and rules quick and found the best way to stay out of the way!

Having no outside help or support Batman applied for a job in the prison kitchen. His job was to wash pots and pans for ten hours out of the day for a measly $16.00 a month. That $16.00 a month would have to get his hygiene items a couple of soups and a box of crackers. To say prison life was hard on him would be an under-statement when Batman thought things couldn't get any worse—it did. A new inmate who went by the name of Bruiser had just come onto the compound. Bruiser was just that, a bruiser. He was 6'5, 240 pounds of muscle and had just transferred from Big Sandy, another maximum prison for stabbing another inmate. Bruiser was from Chicago and the rumor around the prison was that he liked to start trouble.

That wasn't even the tip of the iceberg for Batman, Bruiser had just got hired in the kitchen and was the nephew of Charlie Moe a nickel and dime dope-pusher Batman and Robin had sent to prison in the '70s. Batman found this out the hard way. It was after the noon meal and Batman was in the back of the kitchen performing his job duties, washing pots and pans, when Bruiser came back there.

"What's good, old man? You need some help with these?" Bruiser asked Batman with malice dripping off his tone.

"Nah, youngster I'm good, appreciate it tho."

"Well, I don't appreciate how you got my uncle twenty years in the joint for two dime bags of Cocaine."

"I'm not understanding you youngsta. I don't think I know your uncle."

"You know my uncle, nigga! His name's Charlie Moe from Englewood."

At the mention of the name Charlie Moe, Batman remembered all too well who the small crack pusher was and was now starting to get a little nervous, his silence confirmed it.

"Yeah, I knew you would remember. Listen, and you listen good maggot. I want you to meet me at the warehouse after count, you dig?"

"Man, you got me fucked up," was Batman's reply before Bruiser slapped him viciously across the face, splitting his lip in the process.

Batman tried to fight back but Bruiser was simply just too strong for him, it ended up bad for Batman. He ended up losing his pride as well as his manhood. Batman walked the prison yard with the weight of the world on his back. He was now a true believer in Karma and for all the wrong he'd done on the streets, it was all coming back to him in a 360-degree cipher. He had thirty long, hard years to do with no support and was now a homosexual, he was living hell on earth.

****

Quavon sat in the hospital waiting room, his eyes blood-shot red as he had cried his last tears. Now he just sat in shock. The doctors had told him nothing except that his brother was in surgery and was in critical condition. His heartfelt as if it was about to beat out of his chest. Reggie 'G' was in stable condition, the bullet went in and out and he would be released in a few days. A couple of detectives had come to the hospital to question Quavon about the shooting.

"Mr. Anderson we are investigating the shooting of your brother and your friend. It's best if you know anything about this incident to let us know and to be truthful with us. Do you know why anybody would try to kill you or your people?" Quavon shook his head. "Are you involved in drug dealing or any gang activity?"

"No!"

"Mr. Anderson, we found 5.62-millimeter shell casing at the scene of the crime, that's a very high caliber round. They go through bulletproof vests. It's very extensive firepower Mr. Anderson and whoever was firing that weapon had one thing on their mind, *to kill*. Please help us help you, Mr. Anderson."

Quavon remained silent until his mother Karen come rushing through the hospital doors.

"Where is my, baby?" she asked through her tears as she hugged Quavon tight. Why—what did you do, Quavon? What happened?" She sobbed into her son's chest. Quavon couldn't respond all he could do was console his mother. "Where is my, baby?" Karen pushed Quavon away from her and slapped him across his face. "You did this. You son of a bitch, it's all your fault!" *Slap*!

Quavon was lost for words as his mother's slaps stung his face and her words pierced his heart. The two detectives had to stop Karen from assaulting her son.

In the midst of the emotions and turmoil taking place in the waiting room, the doctor came out. His scrubs were soaked in Davon's blood, it was now complete silence as they wanted to hear about Davon's fate.

"Excuse me, I would like to have a word with the patient's next of kin," the doctor's tone was ominous.

Trembling noticeably, Karen stepped forward and identified herself, "I'm his mother." She wiped the tears that ran down her face.

"I'm Doctor Davis." He guided her away from the others for more privacy. "Ma'am, your son suffered a gunshot wound to the spine. We were able to remove the projectile and stop the internal bleeding. But I'm afraid there's a strong possibility that your son may never walk again."

Karen fell to her knees, as her tears fell from her face.

"I'm sorry, Ma." Quavon just shook his head, he couldn't believe his twin brother would never walk again. At that moment Quavon felt like dying, he wished it woulda been him in that hospital bed instead of his brother

"Can I see him?' Karen asked standing up trying to get herself together. She had to be strong, not just for her but for Davon.

"Right this way ma'am," said Doctor Davis.

Karen walked off with the doctor as Quavon stayed with his feet cemented to the floor. There was no way he could see his twin brother laid up in a hospital bed all shot up. His mother was right, it was his fault. His brother had been shot because of the lifestyle he was involved in. He knew who had made the call, T.B.'s last words were forever embedded in his mind.

"Next time I'ma kill ya ass." T.B. had just crossed the line and it was no turning back for what he had done. He had violated and now his proper punishment was due—*death.*

Quavon made his way toward the hospital exit.

"Mr. Anderson, please let us take care of this, it's been enough bloodshed," one of the offices said.

Quavon heard nothing, the only thing he was trying to hear was the sound of his guns clapping.

S. Allen

CHAPTER 21

YaYo had just come into the unit after being on the yard with Huey all day. YaYo was waiting to get some more tobacco from him, but it was starting to seem like Huey was spinning him. It had been two weeks since YaYo had some product and he was running out of money. YaYo figured he would just give him some space. He walked over to the computers and stood in line waiting to use the email when Pook pulled up.

"What's good, G?"

"Ain't shit, this nigga Huey still playing these monkey ass games with the sauce," YaYo said.

"You know how that shit go. Gotta play niggas for what they worth. Nothing more nothing less."

"You already know, but I'm about to check this email fam. I'ma get with you soon as I'm done."

"Alright, fam."

YaYo and Pook shook hands and YaYo went to the computer. After YaYo logged in on the computer he noticed he had six unread emails. The first one was from a dating site he was on called *Plenty of Fish*. When he read the second one a look of confusion was evident on his face. As he read further into the email the look of confusion turned into a look of grief and YaYo's breath left his lungs.

"Oh my, God," were the only words barely audible when they left his mouth. "No, Davon—no fam, oh my God." YaYo had to step away from the computer, his chest was heaving up and down.

Pook was watching YaYo from across the dayroom, he knew something was wrong, and he briskly walked toward him. "YaYo what's good, homie, you good?"

"My lil' brother, Davon, just got shot." YaYo walked out toward his cell. Once inside his cell, he went to the window and looked out. A tear escaped from the confines of his eyes. "I couldn't protect you, Davon, I'm sorry lil' bro." YaYo loathed himself.

Had it not been for the way he was living on the streets he wouldn't be doing a life sentence in a Federal Penitentiary. YaYo just broke down, he missed his daughter, he would never be there to protect her and teach her. Her first day of school, her graduation—he would miss every part of being a father. He loved his daughter's mother she was his ride or die chick. It was his fault she was a single parent in a heartless world that gave no breaks. He wasn't there to be a perfect man to her or to be her soulmate. Quavon was following in his footsteps, ten toes down in the streets.

If he woulda been on the streets on some positive shit instead of negative. He coulda showed Quavon another way to live life instead of thuggin' and bustin'. He could have molded him into a positive pillar of the community. But he left his brother to the streets to get molded by the murderous environment of Chicago. They had molded him into a cold-blooded goon. YaYo did not want his brother to fall into his footsteps and it hurt his heart, with so much hurt in his heart YaYo did something he hadn't done in a long time, he broke down and prayed.

Pook looked in the cell and saw his homie talking to the Lord. He knew what YaYo was going through because he had been through the same shit, more than once. He knew it was best to give YaYo some space and time to himself. He would check on his homie later.

****

Three Days Later

"Yaton Anderson, report to visitation! Yaton Anderson, out of Charlie Unit report to visitation!"

YaYo was laying on his bunk in a daze when he heard his name over the loudspeaker. He got off his bunk, threw on his Khaki pants and prison-issued boots. He didn't even get fresh for his visit like he usually did. He wasn't in the mood and he was eager to see who had come unexpectedly to visit him. After putting his dreads in a ponytail and buttoning up his shirt, he was out of the cell. Thirty minutes and a strip search later YaYo walked inside the visitation room. It was Sunday so the visiting room was packed to capacity with families coming to see their loved ones.

YAYO

After giving the correctional officer his I.D., YaYo scanned the visiting room until his eyes rested on them. His heart immediately started to flutter, he couldn't believe this, part of him wanted to run over and embrace Shakira while the other part wanted to slap the taste out of her mouth for her disrespect. But when he laid his eyes on his beautiful daughter the anger in his inner beast subsided and only the love for his family was apparent.

Shakira was nervous as well as scared as her baby daddy walked toward them. She sat with her hands folded over her chest. It had been three years since she'd last saw him and yet still his aura and confidence oozed power and respect. YaYo was a born gangsta. The only thing that had changed about him was his dreads, they had grown longer and his body was now covered in tattoos. He was even sexier to her than ever. Shakira stood up to hug her child's father.

"Hey, baby girl. You got so big, look at you!" YaYo said taking his daughter into his arms, planting kisses all over her face. Shamira laughed and YaYo then took a seat at the table leaving Shakira standing there looking stupid.

"Hi, to you too!" she said with a slight attitude but knew she had that coming. YaYo continued to show love and affection to his daughter acting as if Shakira was not even sitting there. "Your mom told me to tell you that she loves you. She also wants to know why you haven't been answering any of our emails?" YaYo continued hugging and talking to Shamira who was all over him. "She said they're moving out of Chicago and going to Milwaukee Wisconsin." YaYo ignored her conversation. "Yaton, why won't you talk to me?" Shakira pleaded, his silence was killing her mentally. "Yaton, I'm sorry baby. I never meant to hurt you, I swear!"

YaYo looked at her with a cold-blooded sneer on his face. "My right-hand man? You're supposed to be my wifey—representing me? You're supposed to be a reflection of me, our relationship and what we've been through. And you go and fuck with my right-hand man?" A tear fell from her eyes.

"Yaton, I am not a normal person. Ever since I fell in love with you. I have buried my momma, I have buried my brother. I have participated in shit that could've got me killed or life behind bars.

Yaton, my life has been on an emotional roller coaster since I have given you my heart. I've given you this beautiful little girl. You have been gone her whole life but, yet she knows who you are. You know why? Because I speak your name to her every day of her life. I'm sorry for what happened with, T.B., and if it makes you feel any better, I did not fuck him. And that's on our daughter, I'm sorry if I'm not as strong as you. But I love you and we want you home. This is killing me, baby. You will never know how much it hurts to not have my daughter with her father." Shakira's tears flowed like the Nile river.

YaYo listened to his wifey pour out her heart and soul. He loved her with all of his being, and he knew she was loyal to him. Even though he was in prison, he had a lot going on in his life. His lil' brother would be confined to a wheelchair for the rest of his life. He was trying to get his sentence overturned and plus, he had to deal with being in prison and the politics that came with it. He needed his family in his life more than ever. He needed their love.

"Shakira, you already know how I feel about what you did. But I'ma take that one on the chin and we gon' move forward. I told you from the jump when I got this life sentence that this was going to be rough. You took this on like a soldier and I love and respect you for that. You've been in my corner from day one and I know where your heart and loyalty is—it's with me. We gon' get through everything, together!"

A smile came across Shakira's lips as YaYo's words melted her heart. She loved him and she was grateful that he gave their relationship another try. YaYo proceeded to tell Shakira about his case and how he was planning to get back in court. Shakira was intrigued by YaYo's knowledge of the law. She could tell that he had been studying and was on his shit. Shakira brought YaYo food from the vending machine, chicken wings, cheeseburgers, and a slice of cheese pizza, YaYo washed it all down with a Lipton ice-tea. It had been awhile since YaYo had some good food so eating during the visit was right up his alley.

Shakira left the visit stronger and with her head held high. She and YaYo made plans for her to come visit once every three months, and she also agreed to contact some criminal lawyers for him. YaYo had a bad feeling in his gut that things were going to get worse for Quavon before they got better.

As he came back from his visit YaYo was more humbled and relaxed. His visit with his family had given him some motivation and he couldn't wait to see Mr. B and check on the status of his case.

As he walked through the prison rec yard en-route to his visit he noticed Huey with a bunch of Mexicans standing by the fence. They were in a semi-circle and Huey was in the middle. YaYo knew it couldn't be too much going on. In Pollock, if there was a problem it always more than likely ended up in bloodshed. One thing for sure something funny was up with Huey, he just couldn't put a finger on it.

Once in the Unit Pook was the first one to say something to him. "What's good homie who came to see you?"

"My baby mama and my daughter," YaYo responded with a smile.

"Oh yeah, that's what's up family. Everything go good?"

"Yeah, bro shit straight. Let me slide up in the cell right quick, I'ma holler at you in a minute. I need to rap with you anyway," YaYo replied and made a b-line to his cell.

Once in the cell, he laid on his bunk. The smell from Shakira's perfume was still on his Khaki shirt. His visit was a good one and he wanted to wear it for a while. Seeing his family leave gave him a lot more motivation, to get home.

S. Allen

CHAPTER 22

Quavon had to get himself back into gangsta mode. He was going to get at T.B. but he had to follow his plan. His twin brother had got shot so the gloves were off. It was on and cracking. Quavon had put down a move to get one of the G.B.C.'s stash house hit and Roccett had sent him a text two days prior. The text read: *//: Get at me when you can got sum for ya.*"

Quavon already knew the business but he had some more business to attend to at the moment. Top Cat had summoned him to meet him at his mansion. So, now Quavon was in a low-key Buick Lacrosse on his way to meet up with Top Cat. Quavon didn't know what Top Cat wanted but whatever it was, he was ready. A Glock 10mm rested in the confines of his black army fatigue, and all-black Air-Max laced his feet. He was in a no-nonsense mood ready to bust my niggas head who jumped out there.

It was 9:30 p.m. when he pulled into Top Cat's circular driveway, parked behind a blue Telsa and hopped out of his whip. Quavon walked up and knocked on the large oak door. After three knocks the door opened.

Behind it was the so-called King of the Westside, Top Cat. "Quavon, come in son."

Quavon stepped inside the massive living room of the mansion. No matter how many times Quavon came to the mansion it always shocked him how large it was.

"Follow me, Quavon, I have some people I want you to meet."

Quavon followed Top Cat down to his fully furnished basement that resembled a small apartment. Waiting in the basement was some of Top Cat's most loyal soldiers, most of them were dressed in all black and all of them had the hunger of wolves in their eyes.

"We are all here for one thing." Top Cat looked around at his crew of Killas. "We are here for the fucking money. Now two of my stash houses have been hit and two of my soldiers were killed behind it."

Quavon tensed up for a minute but he relaxed. This was about the move he put Choppa on. Keeping his composure, Quavon knew he had to play this out like a gangsta.

"Now Quavon you are in charge and command of the security detail, right? Chief of Security, that is your staff titles and duties, am I right?" Top Cat lit his Cuban cigar.

Quavon returned the cold stares of the killers surrounding him before he spoke. "That's correct chief, my staff titles and duties is to secure the foundation you have built. I'm the commanding officer in the streets. I'm aware of the stash house getting hit and I'm conducting an investigation right now as we speak. My intuition tells me that it was an inside job." Quavon scanned the faces of all the men. "Make no mistake the perps that caused this will be punished by death, but as for now we just gon' have to tighten up."

"Man, fuck that ever since you came around it's been some weird shit going on," one of the soldiers said cutting him off.

Without blinking, Quavon pulled the Glock off his waist and shot the soldier in the face. The loud pop from the handgun caused everybody to jump, including Top Cat. The soldier's body hit the floor with a loud *thump* as his brains and blood spilled onto the floor.

"Now like I was saying before I was rudely interrupted, we have to tighten up. Mistakes cost money when Top Cat's money is lost— lives get lost."

Quavon put the hot glizzy back on his waist. Everybody in the basement knew now if they didn't already, that Quavon was a murderer.

Quavon and Top Cat sat on the back porch politicking. "You know, Quavon, it takes a certain kind of man to just walk up and blow a nigga's brains out. You are a different kind of breed. You stay loyal to me and you will go far. That nigga you just shot was suspect to me anyway. He talked way too much for my taste. Bolo and Dime-Bag were loyal soldiers. Soldiers can be replaced but leaders can't. I need you to make sure that what happened in those stash houses never happen again. Do I make myself clear?" Quavon nodded his head. "Now listen next week I have to go to Mexico for a very important meeting. I will need you to accompany me. Will that be a problem?"

"No, sir, if don't nobody got your back—I got you," Quavon said laying it on extra thick.

"That's what I like to hear, Quavon. That's what I like to hear."

Quavon left Top Cat's house in deep thought. The body he'd just caught had him feeling a lil' vexed, he had just taken an innocent life. The man he had killed was a blood sacrifice, to the game. Quavon had Top Cat all figured out, he knew that Top Cat was big on loyalty, as well as greed. He had to crush the nigga in the basement and make Top Cat think it was because of him and his program. The man he'd just killed would just be another body added to his count, which was far from over.

Top Cat wanted Quavon to go to Mexico with him. Quavon already knew that he was taking him to the plug, Mr. Castilino. If Top Cat was going to see Castilino that meant Top Cat was going to drop off some money and in return, Castilino was about to send a truckload of drugs. This was the moment he had been waiting for. He had one week to think of a strategic plan that would bring Top Cat to his knees and the Westside drug trade in his palms.

Quavon pulled up and parked in the back of the Cross-Cross bar on 79th and Vinciness. He took a look at the cars parked behind the bar he knew his team was inside. Quavon had called a mandatory meeting so he could lay out his final plans to his squad. As he entered the smoky basement of the bar, Quavon saw Choppa, Crusha, and Reggie 'G', who held a Sig Sauer 357.

"What's good, my nigga?" Quavon greeted his brothers.

"Same ole same ole. Waiting on you so we can handle this business," Crusha replied.

At that moment, Quavon's phone vibrated in his pants pocket. He looked at his phone he said, "The business." Then sent a text.

Ten minutes late there was a knock at the side door. Choppa grabbed the Calico from under the couch. Quavon put his hand up telling Choppa to fall back and open the door. Roccett stood on the other side with two Nike duffle bags.

"What's good, fam? Come on in." Roccett walked in as Quavon closed and locked the door behind him. "My niggas I want y'all to meet my lil' nigga, Roccett. Loc, Roccett this the Get It Boy Click."

"Sup shawty!" Roccett greeted in his southern slang.

"What's good?" Choppa said still ripping the Calico. Roccett dropped the duffle bags on the floor.

"You come bringing gifts my nigga?" Reggie 'G' asked.

"My niggas' shorty right here family. He is loyal, dependable and definitely about that life. He is my brother same as you, niggas are my brother. His loyalty has been tested over and over and each time he passed with flying colors. My nigga show the family what's in the bags."

Roccett unzipped one of the large duffle bags and dumped some of the contents on the floor. Square bricks of Heroin quickly littered the floor, thirty in total. Next, he grabbed the second duffle bag and repeated the process. This time rubber band stacks of money fell from the bag.

"That's thirty bricks of dope and two-hundred and fifty-three stacks, shawty!" Roccett said as he slung the empty duffle bag.

"I like the nigga already," Crusha said grabbing one of the square bricks examining it.

Quavon just smiled. "This is nothing my beloved ones. This is just a lil' fruit of some of the labor we have been putting in on the streets. Now understand that T.B. and his crew of imposters will have to be dealt with soon. He is the cause for my twin brother being in a wheelchair and for that his life is on borrowed time."

Choppa cocked the Calico chambering a hollow point 9mm round.

"Now this the move my niggas, I have to go out of town next week for an important meeting. This meeting will put us at the top of the food chain. A lot of good brothers have lost their lives for the glorious organization, and more will be lost defending the laws and policies that your organization The Get it Boy Click was built on. My brother was given a life sentence for this and I plan to carry the torch of the G.B.C. Who is willing to carry this torch with me?" Quavon asked his crew.

Crusha was the first to speak. "Quavon me and your brother YaYo go way back, we have come a long way. Too far to let some power-thirsty sucka dismantle what we have built. I will forever be a G.B.C soldier."

Quavon nodded his head in understanding. "Thank you, Crusha. I am my brother's keeper."

Choppa got off the couch, still cradling the assault weapon, he was next to speak. "YaYo gave me a home when I didn't have one. G.B.C. will always be my family. I'm for what's right and if killing these fake niggas is the righteous thing to do then I'm all in. One-hundred shots cocked and loaded. All I know is homicide, it's who I am," Choppa vowed meaning every word that he spoke. He was a street general and Quavon had big plans for him in the near future.

"I'm in it for the love. I love this G.B.C thang we got going on. We are a unit, we are one and one for all. Free YaYo!" Reggie 'G' yelled his loyalty never in question.

Quavon walked up to Roccett with his hands clasped behind his back. "Roccett, you have proved your loyalty over and over, but I think you fail to understand what this is all about. This is about complete dominance, power, and money. You see my brother's vision was for G.B.C to be a superpower in these streets. Never to be tested, to be number one in the streets, in the future and the world. I see my brother's vision through my eyes. A man has to have complete loyalty in his men. Blind loyalty my brother would always tell me when I was younger. We have worked together and had worked well together, but somebody's standing in the way of my vision, my brother's vision."

"Who is that?" Roccett questioned.

"That person is your uncle, Top Cat." Choppa discreetly aimed the Calico at Roccett just in case he felt some kind of way about what his boss was speaking.

Roccett let out a chuckle. "So, you want me to go against my uncle, cuz—my blood family?"

"Remember what I told you about times changing? Well, my nigga, the time's definitely about to change. It's up to you if you are willing to change with them or die starving in these streets," Quavon said his facial expression stone cold.

"First and foremost, Quavon I'm one of Allah's worst children. I fear no man, only Allah. Plus, I'ma rolling twenties Crip. I took a liking from the first time I met you, shawty. You like me in a lot of ways, I bring this back to you out of love and loyalty." Roccett waved his hands over the money and drugs scattered across the floor. "I coulda took it and got ghost. My uncle is in the game. I am in the game as well cuz just like you and your men. The point of being in the game is to win, emotions have no place in this game. Only the strong survive and the ones that's heartless and cold will prevail. Fam what y'all showed me y'all some cold-hearted niggas. I'm fucking with the G.B.C. shawty."

Quavon pulled Roccett into an embrace. "That's what I wanted to hear. Because the G.B.C fucking with you."

After splitting up the money and dope between his crew Quavon laid out his deadly plan. Since some of Top Cat's goons felt some kind of way about him being around he was going to apply a lil' more pressure and spill a lil' more blood. At the same time, he was going to put surveillance on T.B. and once he got back from Mexico he was going to checkmate both his enemies in one swift move. Leaving him the king of the streets. Until then the thirty bricks would be pushed through Top Cat's blocks. Either way, the money must continue to flow.

CHAPTER 23

Back at U.S.P. Pollock YaYo, Sinica and Pook sat in the chow hall eating. It was Thursday so almost the whole prison occupied the dining room due to the fried chicken that was being served.

"Calm down, lil' nigga! The chicken ain't going nowhere. You acting like it's gon' hop off your plate and fly away!" YaYo joked.

"Shit you never know, as big as this bird is, it just might. It's supernatural looking as shit."

The entire table erupted in laughter. While the convicts were demolishing their meals, the deuces went off. Medical staff and Correctional Officers rushed out the administration building with stretchers and pepper spray guna.

"*Fight on Charlie Yard! I repeat fight on Charlie Yard!*" YaYo heard come over the C.O.'s walkie talkie that was standing close by.

YaYo and a few other homies stood up to look out the window.

"Damn they crushing that white boy," Pook said as two white boys from the Aryon Circle proceed to stop another me out until C.O.s ran over to break up the assault.

"That ain't 'bout nothing, long as they didn't put the knife in him, we should be good," Yayo retorted.

After the Correctional Officers broke up the fight YaYo and his homies sat back down and continue their meals. Fights and violent assaults happened daily in Pollock everything was all good until the deuces went off a second time.

"*Fight on Bravo Yard! Fight on Bravo Yard!*"

"What the hell?" YaYo stood back up to look out the window only to witness another assault. The white boys were punishing another one of their people. C.O.s had to now rush to B-Yard.

"Damn this bitch rocking today"

"The white boys must be cleaning up the car," Pook replied.

"*Assault on Alpha Unit! Inmate with weapon! Inmate with weapon!*"

Immediately more staff came running out of the administration building toward Alpha Unit.

"Oh, shit we hit, fam. The deuces went off three times. We for sure going on lockdown." Sinica shook his head, he hated lockdown. His philosophy was you couldn't make no money on lockdown.

"That probably was the white boys in a unit to, huh?" YaYo asked nobody particular.

"Probably, I guess we'll see," Pook replied and went back to crushing his chicken.

YaYo and his homie were stuck in the kitchen. Whatever happened on Alpha Unit had to be serious. They were letting inmates out of the kitchen one by one to be released back to their housing unit and had to be strip-searched first. Correctional Officers stood on the walkway in riot gear and shotguns.

'*This is serious,*' YaYo thought.

After YaYo was strip-searched he made his way back to the unit, something didn't feel right. The sky was grey, and he could feel the tension on the yard as he walked past the guards. They all had serious expressions on their faces. Once YaYo got to the front of his building, C.O. Sanchez and another Correctional Officer was standing there.

"Make sure you go straight to your cell, Anderson," C.O. Sanchez instructed even her flirtatious attitude was replaced with no-nonsense.

"What's going on around here?' YaYo asked as he cleared the metal detector.

"Just put it like this, it's the first one of the year."

"A body?" C.O. Sanchez nodded her head.

'*Damn,*' YaYo thought, he knew for sure they was going to be on lockdown for a minute.

Once in the unit, YaYo went to the computer to send out an email. The unit was already locked down and inmates were secured inside their cells.

"Aye YaYo, check it out real quick!" YaYo knew it was his homie Smoke calling him.

154

After sending out an email to his family notifying them of the prison lockdown state he rushed over to holler at Smoke. He had to make it quick before C.O. Sanchez locked him in his cell.

"What's good, bro?" YaYo asked standing in front of Smoke's cell.

"You know who that was don't you?"

"Hell naw. Who was it?"

"That was your boy, Huey. That nigga dead, bro," Smoke informed him.

YaYo just shook his head in disbelief.

"Mr. Anderson get to your cell now!" C.O. Sanchez yelled standing in front of YaYo's cell waiting to lock him in.

"Man, that's fucked up. I'ma holla at you when we get off lockdown."

"Alright that's a bet, be cool, my nigga."

YaYo made his way up the tier to his cell.

"Next time I say go to your cell, I mean go to your cell," C.O. Sanchez said unlocking YaYo's cell.

YaYo just shook his head and stepped into the small cell. C.O. Sanchez slammed the cell door shut aggressively and locked it. He was really starting to wonder what was up with her. Just recently he was ten inches deep in her, now she had a swift change of attitude toward him. Whatever it was, he would soon find out.

It had been a week and a half and Pollock was still on lockdown status. The prison had conducted interviews for all the inmates in population asking if they knew of the tension on the compound? If they knew what happened and why? They was basically looking for somebody to snitch. There were a lot of real niggas in the FEDs but, yet, still a lot of rats. Guys had hundreds of years and would give up info on a body with the quickness to get out of prison. There was a saying in the FEDs half the niggas in the FEDs told, the other half wish they told.

YaYo was on his 20th set of kick-outs when some mail came sliding under the door. He got up, grabbed his towel, wiped his face and grabbed the mail.

"John Posy, that's you, my nigga," YaYo said and passed it to his celly, Paco.

The second piece of mail was for him. It was from a lawyer's office out in Tennessee. YaYo opened the letter.

Dear Mr. Anderson,

I just received a copy of your 2255 motion, and I have gone over it thoroughly. I can assure you that you have grounds for a new trial due to the information in your motion. Ruth At Law would gladly like to take your case. If you're interested in us taking your case please contact us immediately.

The law firm's contact information was listed at the bottom of the letter in bold font.

YaYo's mouth was open so wide a fly could have flown in it without him even knowing.

He smiled. "That's what the fuck I'm talking about, Mr. B!" YaYo yelled scaring the shit out of his celly.

"What you talking about, my nigga?"

"This what I'm talking about!" YaYo said excited giving the letter to Paco.

Paco could do nothing but smile as he read it. "You about to hit the brick soldier! Told you my nigga good things happen to good niggas." The two gave each other a gangsta pound.

"Who you get some mail from?" YaYo asked hyped up.

Paco passed him the pictures. "She beautiful, fam!" One of the pictures was of Paco's daughter.

"My baby momma sent them. She said she's sorry for leaving me stuck and she wants me in my daughter's life. She said she's with a nigga. She sent five-hundred dollars and some more shit."

"Man, that's what's up fam. They be going out looking for niggas to take our place but when the search come up blank they be realizing we are real as they gon' get. It's a drought on niggas like us! The gon' learn tho," YaYo said with a smirk.

"Square bizness, my nigga."

YAYO

U.S.P. Pollock was a negative, violent place. YaYo remembered the Jamaican on the phone that said it was a cloud of death over the prison. Now looking out of his window he could see the cloud clearly. He had been there for three and a half years and saw more violence than he had seen in the streets of Chicago. YaYo knew he didn't want to die. He didn't want to die in Pollock and be put in a prison cemetery. He had to go home and be a father to his daughter, a son to his mother as well as a brother to his brothers. His family needed him, and he needed them. Running into Mr. B had been a blessing from God. Mr. B had kept his word and it was now possible, he could get back in court and get a new trial. He also remembered the promise he made to Mr. B and he had every intention of keeping that promise, but YaYo also knew the game. Even if you don't want to play anymore. The game will suck you back in and swallow you whole. It was easy to get in jail and hard as hell to get out. Today had been a blessed day for him and his celly. Blessings were pouring in left and right but he had to keep in mind he was still in prison. The devil's playground and the devil and his workers were working full-time. It was time for him to start playing for the streets, his mind was made up that he was going straight. He just hoped and prayed when the streets came calling he wouldn't pick up the phone.

****

Two Weeks Later

The institution was now off lockdown status and YaYo had finally made it to the yard to find out what really happened to Huey. All the time YaYo thought his own people had killed him. Only to find out it was the white boys that punished him. Huey owed the white boy's a few hundred dollars. As you know a few hundred dollars is a lot in prison. The white boys went to holla at the shot caller for Huey's people. The Mexican was already tired of Huey because Huey didn't look out for his people. So, instead, he did business with the other races on the yard. They threw him to the wolves by telling the white boys they had nothing to do with Huey or his is-sues.

The white boys took that as a green light to handle it how they saw fit. They figured they would pull up on Huey one more time in an attempt to get their money from him. When they called Huey in the cell, Huey felt they were pressing him and become slightly ag-gressive. The worst mistake he could have made. The white boys thrashed him. The other fight on the yard was a decoy, so the white boys could put in the work. Huey was murdered in the process, all over two-hundred dollars.

CHAPTER 24

"Now look, shawty, it's gonna be two dudes sitting on the car in front of the house. They're security but all you gotta do is dust them off, cuz. Walk to the door, knock five times and they're gonna open the door because it's the code. All the money is in a bag inside the toilet in the bathroom on the first floor. Once you finish meet me in the back of the house, I'ma be parked waiting on you," Roccett explained sitting in the driver's seat.

They were parked in a dark alley on the Westside of Chicago. Quavon had ordered them to apply some pressure to some of Top Cat's workers. Choppa occupied the passenger seat screwing the silencer on a Glock 26 handgun.

"How many people will be in the house?"

"Three at the most."

"Well, my nigga, I guess I'ma see you in a few minutes. Now watch, Choppa, work." Choppa put on his Chicago White Sox fitted cap and tilted it low over his eyes. He slid out of the car with his Glock tucked snugly behind his back.

Choppa walked between a passageway between two houses and walked down Homan Street when he saw two men sitting on a beat-up Ford Taurus. They seemed to be puffin on some good weed.

'*All the way off point*,' Choppa thought.

"What's good, Joe? Y'all got some of that for sale?" Choppa asked walking up to the two thugs.

"Yeah, we got three for fifty. How many you want?" The one with the long dreads asked pulling out a freezer bag full of twenties.

"I got a hundred, let me get seven for this hunnid."

"A'ight bet," the dread replied eager and thirsty to make the sale.

Choppa used this time to make his move. "Nigga lay on the ground," Choppa sneered pulling his strap and pointing it at the dread head.

The dread head dropped the bag and put his hands up making his way to the ground. Obviously to slow for Choppa. *Psssst*! The

9mm slug hit the dread head front and center of his melon. His partner tried to flee but was too slow. *Psssst! Pssst! Pssst!* Choppa ate his back up with the Glock causing him to collapse on the sidewalk leaking. He walked up and stood over his body, then put one in his head busting it to the white meat.

Calmly Choppa walked up the steps of the front porch and knocked five times, loud music could be heard on the other side of the door as well as the locks being unlocked. A skinny cat with long braids opened the door and was given one to the face. A dark pinkish mist sprayed from the back of his head along with some brain tissue. Swiftly Choppa made his way inside the house with his Glock extended in front of him in search of the other men in the house. He was sitting at the kitchen table bagging up bundles of Heroin. They hadn't heard a thing and was not aware of the three men who'd been murdered in cold blood. Until they saw Choppa enter the kitchen with his Glock pointed in their direction.

"Aaahhh shit," was all he said before the Glock jerked twice in Choppa's hands, hitting the man in his throat and left eye socket.

His brains now dripping down the wall behind him, his man suffered the same faith, shot multiple times in the head. Choppa looked at his work and smiled, satisfied they were no longer breathing. He hurried up and located the bathroom downstairs then removed the toilet lid. Choppa saw the plastic bags filled with cash, grabbed them, made his way to the back door of the house and let himself out.

Sitting in the alley behind the trap-spot was Roccett's Chevy. Choppa briskly walked to the car and got in tossing the bag in the backseat. Without saying a word, Roccett pulled out of the alley and on to Kedzie Street. Roccett knew that Choppa had left Top Cat's soldiers for dead. The smell of death and gunpowder was evident.

"You good, bruh?" Roccett asked breaking the silence.

"Yeah, I'm straight, everything's good," Choppa replied.

The feeling of committing homicide intoxicated him. He was a killa, the streets of Chicago had molded him into a savage beast and putting in work for his gang was out of love. Choppa was TJ reincarnated, his murder game was impeccable and rumors in the streets was his body count was nothing nice, thus the streets naming him, The Grim Reaper of Chicago.

****

It was just a normal day in the Penitentiary for ex-Detective Batman. He was in the kitchen at work, washing pots and pans. He had an hour before he got off it had been a long day. He couldn't wait to get back to the unit so he could shower and lay down. After drying the last pat Batman took off the plastic apron, hung it on the hooks and made his way out of the dish room until Bruiser walked in. From the look on Bruiser's face, he knew what he wanted. Bruiser had been raping Batman for a year, but every time, Bruiser had to fight for it and today Batman was going to fight for his life.

"Where you going so fast, baby girl?" Bruiser growled.

Batman without thinking punched Bruiser in the jaw. Bruiser looked at Batman as a smile came across his lips and he backhanded Batman. Batman threw a three-piece combo to Bruiser's mid-section, but that didn't phase him one bit. Bruiser grabbed him by his throat lifting him off the floor, Batman was about to pass out.

"You gonna make daddy fight for it every time, huh?" Bruiser said as he took his free hand and started unbuckling his belt.

Bruiser threw Batman to the floor as he gasped for air, Batman grabbed his throat attempting to gain his conscious back. Bruiser was about to handle his business with Batman until he felt cold piercing his lower back. Then he felt it again—again—and again. It was at that moment and time he knew he was being stabbed. The pain he felt caused him to drop to his knees.

The man who put the work in walked past him and went to help Batman off the ground. "Come on champ let's get up outta here before the C.O.s come."

Batman and the stranger made their way through the back kitchen and was on time for the ten-minute move. It wasn't until count time that they found Bruiser in the kitchen dish room all stabbed up and almost dead. The prison was placed on lockdown for about thirty minutes, then the captain let it back up. Victorville was hell-bent so the administration cared less about the safety of the inmates and the violence in prison as long as it wasn't toward their staff.

After the yard opened, Batman was on the rec- yard sitting on the bleachers when a man walked up and sat beside him.

The same man who'd saved his life.

"I never got a chance to say thank you for saving my life. Thank You"

"I don't need no thank you's. You see I'm just protecting my investment," the man said with ice in his tone. He was 5'11, 220 pounds of muscle and tattooed from head to toe. His presence was menacing, his name was Sherman.

"What you mean your investment?" Batman probed.

"You see I'm connected to some very powerful people. You ever heard of the Nation Of Islam?"

"Yeah," Batman answered.

"Do you know, Yaton Anderson or YaYo?" A chill ran through Batman's spine as he thought about the drug boss that had his partner killed and attempted to have him killed in the process. "Of, course, you are familiar with him. Young got him a life sentence, am I correct?" Batman remained silent. "My superior is in the same spot with, YaYo. He has taken a liking to the youngsta and believes that you can free him. You get in contact with your attorney and get him to let the government know your investigation was bogus and that the Chicago Police Department deliberately planted false evidence, false statements, and reports against, YaYo. And that you are willing to testify on his behalf that he is innocent. Also that the whole conspiracy against him was made up by you and your co-workers in the Chicago Police Department"

"What happens if I refuse?"

"If you don't do as I say. My man will have you killed on this prison yard. I just saved your life, so pay it forward and save somebody else's life."

Batman thought about it, he was in a no-win situation. He hated YaYo with a passion. YaYo had killed his partner and crippled him. But the work he had just seen Sherman put in was official. He knew when dealing with the *Nation* he was dealing with some real killers. He had no other choice but to do as he was told.

****

Quavon pulled up in front of Mount Sinai Hospital. He hadn't seen his brother since he got shot three weeks ago. He couldn't bring himself to see his twin laid up in a hospital bed paralyzed from the waist down. It hurt his heart to know it was all his fault that Davon got shot in the first place, but he missed his brother dearly and needed to see him. Quavon jumped out of his car, grabbed the Wal-Mart bags from the back seat and walked in the hospital.

After he walked up to the receptionist's desk, Quavon asked, "What room is, Davon Andreson in?" The receptionist looked at her clipboard.

"Sir, Mr. Andreson is in room two-twenty-six."

"Alright, thank you."

"You're welcome, sir," The receptionist said with a warm Colgate smile.

Quavon reached room 226 and slightly knocked on the door before he opened it. Opening The door Quavon saw his brother sitting up in the hospital bed reading some book.

"Took you long enough," Davon said not even looking up from the book he was reading, he already knew who it was. He could feel his twin's presence.

"Yeah, you know, I didn't want to see you like this," Quavon said dropping the bags on the floor.

"What you, reading?"

"I'm studying for this exam I gotta take for school. I'm taking it online," Davon replied.

Quavon was lost for words, even in a hospital bed all shot up, Davon was still adamant about graduating.

"What, you thought some bullets was gon' stop me from getting across that stage? The only thing now is that I can't walk, I gotta roll across the stage." Davon laughed.

Quavon saw nothing funny and a tear fell from his eye. "Bro, I'm sorry, I never meant for this to happen to you." Quavon couldn't understand that with all the shit his twin was going through, he still had his spirits up.

"What you got in the bag, big head?" Davon asked.

Quavon wiped the tears from his eye with the back of his hand. "I went and got you a new Playstation and a few games. I know how you love your games," Quavon said, as another tear about to escape.

"Well, hook it up so I can beat that ass."

Quavon went to hook up the game counsel. Even though his brother was in good spirits seeing his brother paralyzed tore him apart. T.B. was a walking dead man and once Quavon tied up things with Top Cat, T.B. would meet the barrel of his gun.

Quavon enjoyed the time with his brother playing video games and talking about the future. He had even promised he would get back in school and graduate, which made Davon happy. If everything went right with the lick and Top Cat, Quavon and his people would want for nothing. He was ten toes down and about to cash in all his chips. He was either going to come out a winner, or the game was going to be the cause of his demise.

CHAPTER 25

News Anchor

"Thank you for tuning in to WGN News at 10:00, I'm Vanessa Johnson. On today's top story we're reporting a rash of violent murders that have taken place on the city's Westside. Authorities say the killings took place in the Lawndale neighborhood. They say the neighborhood is a high drug traffic area for Heroin and Crack Cocaine, as well as strong gang activity. Two nights ago, two black men were gunned down on a sidewalk, with apparent gunshot wounds to the head. In another house on the same block, three men were found dead inside the home. Police say all five murders were related and would like anyone with my information to please contact the Chicago Police Department."

****

T.B.

"Niggas out West tripping," I said and flicked the remote turning off my 70-inch Vizio T.V. that hung from my wall. I had my own problem, this nigga Quavon was testing my patience and I was tired of playing with him and them faggot ass niggas, Crusha, Choppa and Reggie 'G'. I felt a lil' bad about his brother getting caught up on that bullshit. But in the jungle, it's kill or be killed, I choose to kill. Me trying to get at Shakira was nothing personal toward YaYo. My loyalty to him died when they gave him that life sentence. I know y'all probably calling me a cruddy nigga, but what a nigga thinks about me don't mean shit. I'ma soldier in this game.

I crushed Menace because he was insubordinate. It was going to come a time when he had to pick a side and I already knew he would side with Quavon and the rest of the lames. So, I punished him out the gate. A couple of my spots been getting hit lately and all of a sudden something's telling me Quavon's got something to do with it. He knew everything about how we moved because he used to be one of us. My plug in Miami still hitting me with the brick but I haven't really been concentrating on hustlin' because of this beef with Quavon. But trust and believe I'ma put an end to this shit A.S.A.P! Next time we cross paths I'ma body his ass.

****

The private jet landed in Ciudad Juarez on a small landing trip twenty minutes outside of the city of Mexico. It was Quavon's second time flying. The first time was when he flew to Louisiana to visit his brother at Pollock. The flight was uncomfortable as this one was luxurious and more relaxing. Even then, Top Cat hadn't let him know what the meeting was about. Quavon knew they were down there to cop some work. The two leather briefcases at Top Cat's feet confirmed it.

Top Cat told Quavon that Castilino was a very important man and was the boss of his own cartel, the Medina Cartel. It is because of Castilino that the Westside of Chicago was flooded with drugs. Quavon had put it all together. Top Cat was getting his work on consignment. Kilos upon kilos of Heroin and Cocaine, with all the work Top Cat, pushed over the years he was about to build his own criminal Organization, Ruling it with an iron fist consisting of discipline and murder. Quavon knew he was a key ingredient in Top Cat's army. His bracing and emotionless tactics put fear in the other killers around him so that they feared Top Cat.

After the plane came to a stop in the airstrip, Quavon could see military humvees making their way down the airstrip.

"Look like we got company," Quavon said.

Top Cat stood up patting him on his back. "Those are Castilino's men, here to escort us to him."

Top Cat and Quavon was greeted by one of Castilino's lieutenants.

"Como Estas, Senor. The boss awaits your arrival, right this way please."

"Gracias Amigo," Top Cat responded as he and Quavon followed the lieutenant to one of the humvees.

YAYO

Armed men stood outside the jeeps holding AK-47s and M-16s. They were there to protect the fifty million inside the suitcases Top Cat was carrying.

The ride to Castilino's estate was a bumpy and hot one, riding through the city of Juarez was like coming through a war-stricken country. Chicago was a war zone, but it was nothing compared to Juarez. Top Cat explained to Quavon that Castilino's Cartel was at war with another Cartel that went by the name of Zetas. Hundreds and hundreds of people were killed in the war as they battled over drug territory and Mexico's politics. During the ride through Mexico, Quavon thought he saw a dead body lying in the street.

Top Cat lit one of his Cuban cigars, his diamond Rolex shined off the rays of the sun and he inhaled the sweet smoke for the Cuban. "Quavon, this is what it means to be at the top. You have to get up and go get what you want in life. You must have the ambition and drive, to get to the top."

An hour later they were pulling up into the large circular driveway in front of Castilino's Mansion. Castilino's Estate made Top Cat's mansion look like a small studio apartment. The Humvee pulled up behind a black Range Rover. Castilino and a few of his soldiers stood posted awaiting their arrival. Top-Cat and Quavon stepped out the humvee to greet the plug.

"Como Estas, my friend. Glad you could make it. How was your flight?" Castilino greeted extending his hand to Top Cat.

His diamond pinky ring was the size of a small glacier as his white linen shorts set dropped over his well-toned physique. His salt and pepper hair was neatly combed to the back and he was well into his late sixties even though he didn't look a day past fifty.

"It's good to see you, jefe." He used the Spanish word for boss. "The flight was long, but I'm sure it will be well worth it as it always is," Top Cat replied shaking the plug's hands.

"This must be the fine young man you have been telling me so much about?" Castilino motioned toward Quavon.

"Excuse me for not introducing my youngin'. This is Quavon, Quavon, this is Mr. Castilino."

"Nice to meet you, Quavon. I have heard so many honorable things about you," Castilino said shaking Quavon's hand.

"Likewise." Quavon held a stone face as he greeted the biggest drug lord in the country.

"I'm quite sure you men must be hungry? My wife, Maria has prepared us an exotic dinner. Let us eat so that we can get to the business, shall we?"

"Sounds good to me, I'm starving," Top Cat said.

The men were about to enter Castilino's home until Castilino said something in Spanish to his men. The men immediately turned to Top Cat and Quavon. Then in broken English said, "Hands up, we have to search for you."

Top Cat sat the two briefcases on the ground now holding his hands up.

"You too, amigo, vamanos." The soldier commanded pointing his Mac-11 at Quavon.

Quavon held his hands up allowing the soldier to conduct his pat search. The soldier relieved him of his .40. After the search, Castilino could see the disapproval in Quavon's eyes.

After the large dinner, Castilino's wife cleared the table and went to do some of the house duties, leaving the men at the table to talk business. Castilino went over to a large liquor shelf that was on his wall and pulled out a bottle of Jose Quavo along with three shot glasses After pouring each man a shot he passed them their glasses.

"I would like to make a toast." Castilino raised his glass.

"A toast to riches, power, and longevity." Castilino threw his shot back.

"I can toast to that," Top Cat said and downed his liquor.

Quavon swallowed the smooth liquor and immediately felt relaxed, the warm liquid now floated through his bloodstream.

"Now let's get down to business shall we?" One of his security men came over handing him a white folder, he opened it and said, "Top Cat it says here on my inventory list that you owe for six thousand kilos of Heroin. Do you have that money with you today?"

Top Cat grabbed the two suitcases and placed them on the table. After putting in the code to the lock mechanism he opened both suitcases, revealing stacks and stacks of big faces. "Fifty million American dollars jefe, it's all here."

Castilino smiled, ever since he had been doing business with Top Cat, his money was always right and never short. Quavon had never seen so many dead white men at one time as he stared at the currency in the suitcases. Castilino thumbed through a couple stacks of hundreds.

"You do good business, Amigo. For your hard work and consistency, I am willing to extend my generosity to you. I will drop the price from fifty grand a kilo to thirty grand per key. I am also willing to up your shipment to two hundred extra thousand kilos. Meaning I will be sending you three-hundred thousand kilos. Can you move that much weight?"

Top Cat did the math in his head for three-hundred thousand kilos, he would only have to bring back 90 mil'. After breaking them down he would make a half a million off each key. But with three-hundred thousand bricks he would now be in position to expand his hustle outside of Chicago which he had no problem doing. He would let the birds go for the low and lock down the Midwest, it was a win-win situation.

"I'm a thoroughbred hustla, if anybody can move those bricks it's your man right here!" Top Cat replied.

"Very well, I will have your shipment to you at the same spot in the next forty-eight hours. Have your man on standby."

Quavon was in the back of Castilino's Mansion standing by the large pool, smoking on some good grade marijuana that Castilino had given him to smoke. He couldn't believe Top Cat trusted him enough to put him front seat in his business like that. Quavon knew this was going to be the lick of his life. The only problem was he didn't know where the shipment was going to be dropped off. He had to find out so he could put his team on point. Top Cat was making moves, three-hundred thousand bricks was a lot of work and definitely worth taking his life for.

Quavon's thoughts were interrupted when Castilino came on the patio. "Como Estas, my friend. You good?"

"Yeah, I'm good. Just getting my thoughts together," Quavon said.

"You know your boss speaks highly of you? He says you are ahead of your time." Quavon took a pull from the blunt and inhaled the smoke in his lungs before he passed the weed to Castilino.

Castilino took a strong pull. "The only way a man can make it in this game, Mio, is for him to be his own boss. Always remember that and you will go far." Castilino gave Quavon a jewel as he blew smoke from his nostrils.

For whatever reason Castilino gave him game. He was going to take it for what it was worth. Castilino was a boss in every aspect. Through his power, he was able to distribute millions of kilos all over the world. He had a small military at his beckoning call and millions. Whatever he was doing was definitely working.

Quavon had plans to be the next jefe and if everything went right, his dreams and ambition would flourish into something great. For him and the G.B.C. but first, he had to find out where the dope was getting dropped and he had just the person who might have known. This was going to be like taking candy from a baby!

CHAPTER 26

Choppa, Roccett, Reggie 'G' and Cruhsa sat patiently in a black tinted Yukon Denali truck. They all sported blue jackets with bold yellow letters on the back that read F.B.I. Inside their holsters rested fully automatic Glock 17s each with high capacity magazines. Quavon had gotten the drop location from Roccett. The drop was going to be made at a warehouse off 26th and California Street. In an area populated by a lot of Hispanics. The plan was simple, Quavon would be at the warehouse with Top Cat waiting for the truck. The truck would be en-route and have to pass through 26th and California, that's when the G.B.C posing as U.S. Marshals would pull the truck over. Then snatch the kilos by any means necessary and take it to the designated location. The move had to go as planned.

It was 11:30 at night when the 18-wheeler turned down 26th Street on the city's Southside.

"Look alive, my niggas. It looks like these our boys, right here," Crusha said sitting up in the driver's seat of the Denali.

Reggie 'G' double-checked his clip before he stuck it back in the weapon and chambered a round into the chamber. "Showtime, my nigga."

The semi drove by the Denali. Crusha started the truck and pulled into traffic behind the 18-wheeler, after putting a police siren on the dashboard he activated the reds and blues.

"Y'all think they going go for it?" Roccett asked but answered his own question when he saw the semi pulling over. "Alright, y'all know the drill. Me and Reggie gon' snatch the rig. Choppa jump in the front seat and meet us back at the spot."

"Let's get it," Crusha said putting the fake badge around his neck as he and Reggie got out the truck.

The Mexican in the passenger's seat was sweating profusely as Crusha walked up on the driver's side of the truck showing his badge and hand on his Glock.

"F.B.I step out of the truck please—nice and slow."

The Mexican acted as if he didn't speak English, his partner in the passenger seat was wanted for murder in West Texas and would be damned if he got caught with thousands of Kilos of Heroin on top of that. He reached for the Draco AK-47 on his side of the seat.

"I'm not going to ask you again! Step out of the truck."

"Okay, mi friend." The Mexican opened the door and proceeded to step out of the truck.

Reggie 'G' had his hammer pointed at the passenger. "Passenger step out of the truck with your hands up," Reggie 'G' instructed.

The passenger's hesitation would be the cause of his ruin.

"Bust 'em, fam!" Crusha said.

Boc! Boc! Boc! The Glock spit as Reggie 'G' pulled the trigger hitting the Mexican up with hollows. His body fell out of the truck along with his rifle.

"Please my friend, don't kill me," The Mexican said standing and shaking in front of Crusha.

"Oh, now you speak English, huh?" *Boc!* "Welcome to the Chi," Crusha said before squeezing the trigger -- *Boc! Boc! –*

putting two more shots in the Mexican's head, sealing his fate.

Crusha jumped in the driver's seat of the semi and Reggie 'G' jumped in the passenger seat. After pulling the truck onto California Street the Denali pulled off following the bricks. The Get It Boy Click had snatched the truck full of Heroin and left two Mexicans in a puddle of their own blood.

Top Cat's two-thousand dollar Alligator shoes could be heard clicking against the pavement as he paced back and forth. His nerves were in overdrive. The shipment was running two hours late which never happened before.

"Well, you tell that motherfucking nephew of mine to get his ass to the warehouse immediately," Top Cat sneered into his phone before disconnecting the call.

He had been trying to reach Roccettt but to no avail. He had even contacted Castilino only for Castilino to tell him he would check on the situation and call him back which made him more frustrated, he wanted answers.

"I'm quite sure it has to be some kind of explanation for this," Quavon said.

Four of Top Cat's soldiers stood with assault weapons slung over their shoulders.

"I know one thing, that motherfucking truck better show up in the next thirty minutes or we on our way back across the border."

Just as Quavon thought, Top Cat would place blame on Castilino for the truck not arriving. All he needed now was to get Top Cat away from his goons for one minute and he would end this deadly game he was playing with Top Cat. Quavon used his authority to take control of the situation.

"Aye my nigga, I need y'all to sweep the premises. I gotta feeling that truck gon' pull up in a minute." Quavon wanted to be on point.

The goons looked at Top Cat for confirmation. "Y'all heard what the fuck he said. He's the Chief of Security, follow his orders." The goons walked off to follow the orders that were given.

"Let me find out they not respecting your position. I might have to find me a new chief of security," Top Cat said stress and worry were all over his face.

"Nah, sometimes niggas just need a lil' motivation." Quavon discreetly pulled the silenced .380 from his back. It was now or never. "You know Top Cat you had a long run in the game. You shoulda bowed out gracefully instead you let your greed be the cause of your downfall."

Top Cat turned around slowly, now facing an armed Quavon. "So, this how you gon' play it, huh? I bring you to the table to eat and you bite the hand that feeds you? You got the truck, huh?" Quavon nodded his head and raise the .380 now pointed at Top Cat's head. "I must say you played your cards right, I respect that."

"Get on your knees," Quavon sneered chambering a round into the chamber as Top Cat did what he was told.

"We will meet again, Quavon. You are destined to hell! Just know when you get there, I will be sitting on the throne."

Pssst! A hollow-point round found home in Top Cat's cranium, blowing his brains out. Top Cat died with his eyes open. They always said when you die with your eyes open, you deserved it. At that moment the goons came back into the warehouse. "Y'all niggas get rid of this piece of shit."

The goons came over and did what they were instructed to do. They had been a part of the plot from the beginning. Quavon had promised them riches beyond their dreams if they sided with the G.B.C. Of, course, their greed made them switch up. Loyalty was nowhere in their bloodline. So, while they wrapped up Top Cat's soulless body, Quavon walked up and issued them all headshots. Deceit and betrayal had no room in his camp.

Later that night, Quavon and his loyal G.B.C. squad were at a low-key warehouse in Markham Illinois. They had opened the 18-wheeler that was packed to capacity with a 100 percent uncut Heroin, three-hundred thousand kilos worth. The entire G.B.C. was at stake. Quavon jumped off the bed of the truck with two bricks in his hands.

"My niggas we did it. We about to lock the city down. Sky's is over the limit and it's because of y'all loyalty, hard work, and love that made this all possible. I love y'all, fam! And know I'm always gon' be here for y'all. It's time for us to get to the top and stay at the top."

"That's what I'm talking about!" Choppa said.

"This the plan my dudes. We about to get on some real get down or lay down shit. It's a new day. This G.B.C we will not be tested, either these niggas buy dope from us, or they sell nothing. They violate that they pay with their lives."

The Got It Boy Click was about to get on some real hustle shit. They had 300,000 kilos to move and the only way for them to do that was to have complete dominance over the streets. Quavon knew that with his crew, he could pull it off. He knew he was on his way, but he had one more loose-end he needed to tie up. He still hadn't caught up with tough ass T.B.

****

Three Months Later

"I'm not gonna ask you again you, old bitch. Make the call," Choppa growled putting the gun under the old lady's chin.

She had made the grave mistake of giving birth to T.B.'s mother, being his grandmother. Quavon sat on the couch in the lady's living room overseeing the madness. He was tired of playing with T.B. so once he found his people's information, he devised a plan. The internet was a motherfucka. The old lady fearing for her life called her grandson. She didn't know what these violent men wanted with her daughter's son, but whatever it was it wasn't good.

The phone rang three times before he answered. "Hello?"

"Tobias these men want to—" Quavon snatched the phone from her.

"What's good, Killa?" Quavon sneered.

"Who the fuck is this?"

"This the nigga that got a gun to your grandma's head. Bitch ass nigga you shot my brother. So, I'm definitely trying to see you."

"Quavon, man don't hurt my granny. She ain't got nothing to do with this," T.B. pleaded

"Pussy, my brother didn't either. Nigga meet me on 39th and Prairie across from the Ida B. Wells projects. You not there in thirty minutes I'ma pop this old bitch." Quavon ended the call. T.B. had underestimated Quavon and had just found out that Quavon was playing for keeps.

****

CHICAGO TRIBUNE

"At 11:00 last night, an elderly woman was found shot to death in her home on the 8500 block of Winchester. Police say the woman was found by her daughter late last night. Police would like anyone with information to please notify the Chicago Police Department. At 2:30 a.m. a body of an unidentified male was found in a dumpster

on the City's Southside. Authorities say the man was shot in the head in an alley in the Ida B Wells Projects. Police have no suspects and would like anybody with any information on this homicide to contact Chicago Police."

"Damn, they out there tripping," YaYo said to himself as he read the local section of the Chicago Tribune. The local section of the paper was nothing but unsolved murder and violence. The city had reached the highest murder rate in the country with 850 murders and the year wasn't even over. Statics proved that the city of Chicago had more killings than the war being fought in middle East Iraq. This murderous city taking in the name, Chi-Raq. All YaYo could do was shake his head. His brother had been confined to a wheelchair because of gun violence in Chi-Raq and his brother, Quavon was in the battlefield, issuing his share of death in the city.

"What's in the paper, youngster?" Mr. B asked as he read the letter, he'd just received in the mail earlier. He and YaYo were sitting at a table in the dayroom.

"It's bad out there, Mr. B, old ladies getting killed. Young black men getting found shot in dumpsters. It's like Genocide out there."

Mr. B took off his glasses. "It's because those young men don't have anybody to teach them that killing and selling dope is not right. All the leadership is locked up behind these walls. We need the leaders back on the streets." Mr. B handed the letter he was reading to YaYo

"What's this?"

"Just read it, son."

Bernard,

My comrade in arms, I am writing to you with love and respect. In hopes that this scribe reaches you In good health and blessings as it should. As far as that issue you told me to handle with that individual. It has been taken care of. He has contacted his lawyer and the proper associates as I have witnessed. We are currently waiting on a response. Our movement is moving graciously forward as our superiors and higher-ups have wanted it. Our Nation is strong and together we will grow. Tell YaYo I send my love and respects. Power to our people, Sherman.

YAYO

YaYo couldn't believe it. "This means Batman's gon' get me out this jam?" YaYo asked.

"Insha Allah, my brother. If everything goes right, you could be on your way home within a year. Now all you have to do is get back up with the lawyer and put him on your case. All the hard work has been done. If the cop testifies on your behalf as I know he will. It's an open and shut case, they will either free you or knock your time down from that life sentence and give you something you can deal with. Either way, it's a win-win situation."

YaYo's heartbeat sped up at the thought of going home. He was so close to his freedom he could smell it! If Batman testified on his behalf he was a free man.

"Mr. B, I just want to thank you for helping me out," YaYo said genuinely from the heart.

"Yaton, don't thank me with your words. We have a Nation of young black men out there with no direction in life. If you want to thank me. Thank me with actions and do all that you can to give as many as these young black men some direction."

YaYo extended his hand to Mr. B. "You got that, Mr. B. On my word I'ma do all I can and my word is my bond."

Mr. B shook YaYo's hand. "Then I want to thank you, my brother."

****

Correctional Officer Sanchez was at home in Shreveport Louisiana. Instead of being at work she was over the toilet throwing up. For the last couple of weeks, she had been waking up sick, not to mention her period was late, so a pregnancy test sat on the bathroom sink. She was now awaiting the results. She hadn't had unprotected sex for a while until her lust for YaYo had her panties to her ankles and him pumping in and out of her walls without a condom. She knew without a doubt that she was pregnant and the two lines on the pregnancy test confirmed it.

"Shit!" C.O. Sanchez cursed herself for being so stupid.

There was no way she could bring this child into this world. YaYo had a life sentence, he would never be able to be a father. But another side of her wouldn't let her have an abortion. She couldn't kill her firstborn but she didn't know if she should tell YaYo about her pregnancy. She was confused, the only thing she knew to do for the moment was to get on her knees and pray for God to give her the answers to her dilemma.

CHAPTER 27

One Year Later

Quavon sat in the backseat of a Maybach as his driver slid the exotic vehicle through Chicago's mid-day traffic. Taking a pull from the strawberry Kush, Quavon held the smoke in his lungs until his chest began to tighten up. He looked at his *Cartier Moen Series* watch that was flooded with diamonds and saw he was running late for a meeting he had with a local rapper that went by the name, Lil-Dunk. Quavon was promoting a new movie called Chicago's Beast and wanted Durk to do the soundtrack to the movie.

In One-year Quavon had made it to the top! He promoted parties. He had real estate all over the Midwest and parts of the South and had landed a deal with Lion Gates Films. He was the *boss* as well as C.E.O. for The Get It Boy Click and now controlled the distribution market for the entire Midwest. Milwaukee, St. Louis, Kansas City, Detroit, Cleveland, and Flint Michigan were just a few of his strongholds. He was the cause for sixty-five percent of the Heroin and Cocaine in Chicago, so he chose Chicago as his headquarters.

Even T.B.'s old plug had made a few moves with Quavon on some bricks. He was now the God of the dope game. Quavon's rules and demands were almost never tested. His rules were buy from him and the G.B.C or you couldn't sell drugs in Chicago at all. His recipe and discipline were simple, murder. The majority of Top Cat's soldiers were now under the Get It Boy Click's control and Quavon's laws of the land.

Those that weren't their bodies were found all over different areas in the State of Illinois, with their heads split. It was only one way. Get down or lay down! Quavon now sat on the throne and had been crowned King of Chi-Raq!

It had been an hour and a half since Batman was led off the stand in handcuffs and leg irons and shackles. He was brought to Chicago from Victorville California to testify on YaYo's behalf. Batman testified that all the reports, investigation and evidence placed on YaYo was bogus. When the prosecutor asked why he framed YaYo, Batman stated that YaYo had basically got away with murder for killing the five-year-old girl and only served seven years in Prison. Only to get out of jail and continue killing and living as a criminal. Batman further explained his parent's murders and justice wasn't served. Telling the judge he despised gang members and the drug dealers targeting YaYo was a personal vendetta.

The prosecutor's key witness was Butterball. Butterball was the one that laid the cement over YaYo's sentence, but now it seemed as if Butterball had literally disappeared from the face of the earth. Because Batman had changed his statements and Butterball was nowhere to be found the United States Government had to put it in the jurors' hands and to decide YaYo's faith. The 2255 motion prepared by Mr. B exploited all the deceit and lies in YaYo's case, to the highest of exploitation.

Now YaYo sat next to his lawyer, Mr. Ruth awaiting the outcome of the verdict. YaYo's mom Karen sat in the front row seat with her hands clasped in front of her face silently praying to God for the verdict to come back not guilty. Shakira sat next to her holding her daughter, her heart was beating at a thousand beats per second. She admired her child's father as he sat dressed in an Armani three-piece suit. His long dreads were tied in a neat ponytail down his back. The 1,500 ostrich loafers matched the pinstripe grey suit. Standing trial fighting for his life would be worth living. She would cherish and cater to her man.

Davon sat in his wheelchair, it hurt his heart to see his brother in shackles. He hadn't seen YaYo in four years and missed his brother dearly. Davon was scheduled to graduate college next week and he prayed YaYo was a free man to see him get his college diploma.

The time YaYo had been waiting for had finally arrived. "All rise," the bailiff said as he and the jurors came out of the chambers after deliberations. A thin, black woman with rimmed glasses stood holding a piece of paper with YaYo's future on it. She stepped to the front of the courtroom.

YaYo held his head up like the boss that he was.

CHAPTER 28

YaYo stood next to his attorney as the verdict was read that would determine if he would be free to continue living his life, or if he would grow old and be laid to rest in a Federal Penitentiary.

"On count one of the indictment. We the jury find the defendant not guilty."

YaYo let out a sigh of relief as the verdict continued to be read. Shakira was a nervous wreck as sweat beads began to be visible on her forehead.

"On Count two of the indictment, murder in the first degree. We the jury find the defendant not guilty."

YaYo could see his freedom through his Prada frames. "On count three of the indictment, possession of a firearm by a felon. We the jury find the defendant guilty."

YaYo shook his head side to side. He knew that he wouldn't be walking out of that courtroom and into the warm embrace of his family. Even in his disappointment, YaYo had to give thanks to the man above. The two counts he was found not guilty of were the most serious. The ones that carried the life sentence. When the feds raided his house they confiscated the PLR-16 assault rifle and already being convicted of a felony he wasn't able to carry or own a firearm so the 922G weapon indictment stuck with the FEDs. The maximum time YaYo could receive on the gun charge was 120 months, ten years. Off his sentence, he would have to serve eight years and six months. He'd already served almost four years in on it. The worse case he would have to serve four more years.

'*Four years sounds a lot better than life,*' YaYo thought.

"Okay, Mr. Anderson, what this means is you have been found not guilty on Count One and Count Two of your federal indictment and found guilty on count three which is possessing a firearm while being a felon or being on probation or parole. This charge carries a maximum sentence of ten years in prison, a twenty-thousand dollar fine and an assessment fee of one hundred dollars that is to be paid immediately. Do we have a recommendation from the government at this time?" The judge asked turning his attention to the District

Attorney who stood up and took a sip of the water before she replied to the judge.

"Yes, your honor, the United States government recommends that Mr. Anderson be admitted to the Bureau of Prison for a confinement time of one-hundred and twenty months for the federal charge of possessing a firearm by a felon. This sentence is to be served in a maximum-security facility. At this point and time, Mr. Anderson is housed at the United States Penitentiary Pollock in Louisiana. It is the recommendation of the Government that Mr. Anderson continues to be housed at this facility without the opportunity to transfer to a lower level facility due to his gang influence Mr. Anderson, is to have no ties or communication with the Get It Boy Click," The D.A read from her yellow legal pad.

The judge fixed his rimmed glasses on his long-crooked nose. "Mr. Anderson, I see it has been a change of events? I don't know how but I agree with the D.A. that a sentence of ten years is appropriate for the indictment and the sentence of ten years is a good solution to further protect the community. Mr. Anderson, you have gotten a pretty light sentence here today. Had it not been for count one and two being dismissed here today you would have been in Federal Prison a lot longer than eight years. So as far count three of the indictment '922 G' possessing a firearm by a felon. I hereby sentence you to the Federal Bureau of Prison for a term of one-hundred and twenty months, three years of supervised release will be followed as well as a twenty-thousand dollar fine and a one-hundred-dollar assessment. That is to be paid immediately. Mr. Anderson is to be returned to the B.O.P. immediately." The judge commanded and slammed down the gavel. YaYo was led out of the courtroom for the second time. This time leaving his family disappointed at the outcome of his court proceedings.

After returning from his court date YaYo was called over the intercom for a visit. He had already set up a visit with Shakira after court. YaYo was led to the room where there were six visiting booths, it hurt him that he wouldn't be able to hug his family but he had to keep his emotions in check and be strong like the soldier he is in front of his people. When he sat behind the booth he couldn't believe who was on the other side. He was only expecting Shakira to be on the visit but on the other side was not only Shakira but his mother Karen, his grandmother Honey and his beautiful daughter Shamira.

Seeing his daughter YaYo's chest tightened as he was unable to stop the warm tear that escaped from his eyes. He wanted to break the glass that separated him from his loved ones. Shamira looked at her father and reached for him like the glass was not even there which only made Shakira get emotional and tears cascaded down their cheeks. YaYo got himself together, sat on the small stool in the visiting booth and grabbed the phone. Shakira grabbed the other one.

"What's up, sweetheart?" YaYo cooed into the phone.

Shakira grabbed Shamira from her grandmother, sat her on her lap and put the phone to her ear.

"Hey, baby girl! You're getting so big, Mira!" Shamira smiled and placed her tiny hand on the glass trying to touch her father, which only broke YaYo's heart as he touched the glass. "Daddy loves you, baby girl."

"I love you, daddy. Daddy, you come home today?"

YaYo's voice was caught in his throat as he struggled to find the words to say to his only child. "Shamira, daddy will be home soon, but daddy can't come home today okay?"

The look on Shamira's face let him know he had just crushed her spirits that in return crushed his. She began to cry, Yayo looked into his daughter's eyes with a stern look.

"Shamira, listen to your daddy and stop crying," said Shakira.

The little girl sniffled back her tears and dried her eyes with the backs of her hands.

"Shamira, I need you to be a big girl and stop crying. Daddy will be home real soon. Until I come I'm going to see you every month. Mommy gonna bring you to see me, okay?" Yayo tried to soothe her.

"In an airplane, Daddy? I get on the airplane like mom?" Shamira asked full of excitement.

"Yes, baby, you can get on the airplane, but you have to be a big girl?"

"Okay, daddy" Shamira replied before she waved and hopped off her mother's lap.

Shakira grabbed the phone with a sad look plastered across her face. "What's up with you, my Queen, you okay?"

Shakira wiped the tears from her face. "These people be on some bullshit. What they mean ten years baby? You was supposed to come home to us today."

"Baby everything doesn't always go as planned. But look at it like this is a blessing from God. These crackers had given me a life sentence. They had made me the walking dead. Shakira my out date read deceased baby, it was over. Now we have a chance. I can come home, raise my daughter, have more kids and grow old with you. All that shit before today was non-existent. I pull four more years and I'm home, baby—four more years," YaYo repeated making sure his queen understood.

Seeing her daughter's father so strong in the midst of turmoil only gave her strength, they were one.

"I love you, Yaton!"

"I love you too, baby! We got this shit. This ain't nothing to a boss," YaYo said his confidence oozing from his being.

"Umm excuse me can I have a word with my son?" Karen said with a fake attitude.

Shakira stood up passing Karen the phone so she could speak to her son. "How you holding up, son?"

"I'm good, mama. How are you?" YaYo asked noticing all the grey hair on his mother's head.

The dark circles under her eyes let him know that she had been worrying and stressing. He knew he was the cause of ninety-five percent of her stress. Karen knew the things that went on in Pollock and was always worried about her son and his well-being.

"I'm good, son. Every day I wake up is a blessing because everybody don't wake up, Yaton. So, every morning you wake up make sure you thank God. Now explain to me what them white folks was in there talking about. Because you know your mama don't understand all that legal talk."

YaYo looked in his mother's eyes with a smirk on his face before he said, "Mmmm, I don't have a life sentence anymore! I only got to do four more years, then I'm coming home."

Karen smiled showing all thirty-two of her pearly white teeth. "I told you, son, always that God is good. He will never put nothing on you that you can't bear."

YaYo saw only half-truth in what his mother spoke as he thought about all the men in Pollock with no out dates and the tiring conditions they were forced to live in. He also thought about Mr. B and how he was placed in his life when he needed him the most. Had it not been God placing Mr. B in his life, he would be just part of the seventy-five percent of inmates doing hard time in U.S.P Pollock with no hope or faith in getting out. So, he thanked God for his blessings.

His mother continued, "You know Davon was expecting you to be at the graduation."

YaYo put his head down at the thought of him being confined to a wheelchair. "How is my brother doing, mama?"

"Well, I'm glad to say that Davon is doing good. He has been going to physical therapy and guess what, Yaton—"

"What, ma?"

"It's a good chance that Davon will walk again."

YaYo smiled, he knew Davon's character and knew his lil' brother wouldn't take being in a wheelchair for the rest of his life. He had too much drive, too much ambition as well as a strong heart. He had the heart of a lion and a brain like Einstein.

"What about, Quavon, mama. How he out there doing?"

An unpleasant expression came across her face of the mentioning of the son. "Yaton, Quavon, is a replication of you in so many ways. He is following in your footsteps Yaton. Quavon is out there doing God knows what. I hear his name so much in the beauty shop. Sometimes when the phone rings, I think it's going to be somebody calling me to come identify his body. Chicago is so messed up, baby. It is so much killing out here at times, I don't even want to leave the house. I know it sounds crazy, but sometimes I wish Quavon would get put in prison. At least I would know where he is at night. If I was to get that call, Yaton, I would go crazy. That's a mother's worst nightmare, to bury her child."

YaYo knew how his mother was feeling to have one child in federal prison and another in the streets racing to the grave, not to mention the baby in a wheelchair. YaYo had left his mark on the streets of Chicago and even though he was no longer in them, those associated with or a part of him and the venomous life he lived were still suffering from the actions and the decisions he made.

"Mama don't worry about Quavon, he gon' turn his life around. He just going through a phase, sometimes he might have to learn the hard way. But trust and believe I'm going to talk to him and give him some words at advice."

"Please do son, because he definitely needs it along with a lot of prayer."

"Who the lil' lady over there?" YaYo said nodding toward his loving grandmother, Honey.

"Ma, your grandson wants to talk to you. I love you son and always remember give everything to God and let him do the rest."

"I love you too, ma."

Honey grabbed the phone from her daughter and sat on the stool facing her grandson. "Praise the Lord, Yaton."

"Praise the Lord, granny."

"Yaton every night I pray for you. I pray for your safety and your well-being. I pray for you to change your life. Grandson, you don't know the blessings that you have. You have a beautiful daughter who needs you in her life. She needs you to be out here, to protect her as she grows into a beautiful flower. Shakira needs you, Yaton our family needs you. So, please do what you have to do to come home to us, grandson. Come home with a plan, because a person with no plan only plans to fail. Always remember that."

Yaton continued to visit with his loved ones until the guard hit the door letting him know to wrap his visit up. Today had been a blessed day. Even though he wasn't released back into society he knew he wouldn't die in captivity. Seeing his family and hearing them express how much they need him out there only gave him more motivation to change his life for the better and be a positive role model for his family as well as the community. When he went back to Pollock he was going to enroll in every educational or vocational program that the prison had to offer.

He also had been thinking about Mr. B and how he always invited him to hear members from the Nation of Islam speak. He was definitely going to go check that out. On his way back to his cell block, Yaton thought about calling Quavon. He knew his lil' brother was far too gone in the streets, but little did he know Quavon had leveled up in the streets and far too gone was just an understatement.

S. Allen

CHAPTER 29

"Damn girl suck this motherfucker," Quavon grunted as Asia a chick he met out of town, tried her best to deepthroat him. They were at the Trump Plaza downtown Chicago on the 50th floor. Asia was 5'4, 135 pounds, red-bone with big-titties and a phat ass. Asia had been on Quavon's hills the minute he stepped inside club Real on Bil Street downtown Memphis. Quavon and Roccett had gone to Memphis, Tennessee to pick up some money from one of the work-ers who went by the name of, T. Clay and had decided to hit the club after they handled their business.

It had been a year since Quavon and the G.B.C. hi-jacked the semi-truck that was loaded with 300,000 kilos of uncut Heroin. Quavon and his team had managed to lock down the drug trade in the Chi, by eliminating the competition. Quavon approached high-level drug-dealers throughout the city, the proposal was to either buy weight from the G.B.C or forfeit your rights to make money on some streets that Quavon had claimed. Some proposals were re-jected by those that chose to go against the grain. Those rejections were frowned on by Quavon and the G.B.C so pistols and assault rifles were used to make sure the G.B.C laws and policies were ad-hered to.

The G.B.C had blocks and trap spots throughout the city that did numbers as high as 100 gees a night. Not only did Quavon and his crew have the city in their palms but they also controlled other areas in different states in the vice-grip as well. Memphis, South Carolina, Baltimore, and eventually Quavon started working with some get money niggas out of D.C.

Quavon and the Get It Boy Click was running through the dope at an alarming rate due to the low cost of the uncut bricks. In an era where keys of Heroin were going for eighty-five thousand, Quavon fronted the dope for forty gees a brick as the quality of the product was unmatched. In any city, knowing his product would run low, Quavon needed a steady, consistent plug and made a decision that would cost him his life. Or take him to the top of the food chain.

Quavon watched as his thick long dick slid in and out of Asia's tight pussy while he held her thin waist slamming into her from the back. The fifth of Apple Ciroc and the two blunts of Sour Diesel Kush had his stamina all the way up.

"Baby, baby—it' so big. Quavon—I feel you in my stomach," Asia moaned with her face in a pillow.

Yo Gotti's Lifestyle blasted through the speakers of the Bose entertainment system that was embedded inside the wall. Quavon's chiseled athletic frame was glistening from sweat. He turned Asia around on her back, Quavon put her thick toned thighs over his shoulder and slid up in her missionary style. Asia could feel the thick veins in his dick while he proceeded to punish her juice box all the while squeezing her double Ds. The loud music in the room did little to muffle the sound of sweaty flesh slapping against each other. Quavon's balls smacking against Asia's ass drove her crazy. He was hitting her spot with each stroke. Asia was falling for him she knew she was getting fucked by a boss nigga and the thought of it all made her climax.

"Oooh shit, Quavon!" Asia gripped Quavon's sweaty ass cheeks as she creamed all over his monstrous meat.

Quavon continued to punish Asia sexually before he felt his volcano about to erupt as he speeded up his stroke. Asia's pussy juices coated his inner thighs. Quavon pulled out of Asia and grabbed a handful of her hair, putting his dick in her mouth. Asia welcomed his dick and used two hands to jerk his dick, as his big balls slapped against her chin.

"Fuckkk!" Quavon yelled forcing his dick further down Asia's throat trying to touch her tonsils.

Asia was doing good with the gag reflex until Quavon shot his thick warm nut down her throat impregnating her esophagus. Asia swallowed as much as she could, what she couldn't escaped from the corner of her mouth dripping down and coating her big titties.

Quavon had just dozed off into a slight nap when his iPhone 6 vibrated on the dresser next to him. He grabbed the phone and looked at the caller I.D. He saw the number was restricted, Quavon did not like answering restricted but this time his curiosity got the best of him, so he answered.

"Hello?"

"You have a collect call from—YaYo. To accept this call press five to block this call press seven."

Quavon sat up with his back against the headboard and pressed 5 on his smartphone.

"What's good, fam?" Quavon greeted happy to hear from his brother.

"Same ole shit. What's good with you?"

"Ain't shit. Just trying to get it how I live," Quavon replied eyeing Asia's phat, naked ass while she slept.

"So, I heard. Listen, man, I already know Ma told you what happened in court."

"Yeah, I'm already hip, bro. It's a blessing to know you ain't gone grow old in there. Just know I'ma have shit laid for you when you touch down. Your seat atop the throne awaits you," said Quavon.

"Nah, bro, I'm out. I'm not living that life no more," vowed YaYo. He heard his brother sort of chuckle. "Quavon, I'm serious. We're stressing the shit out of Mama. We gotta—"

"We ain't gotta do shit!" Quavon cut him off. "All the shit I been through these past four years -- nigga, I'm in it till the end. You wanna come out here on that preaching shit, then that's what you do. But I'm doing *me*, fam." Quavon hung up the phone, leaving YaYo talking to a dial tone.

At that point, YaYo knew that his little brother's soul belonged to the devil.

S. Allen

CHAPTER 30

Back Inside U.S.P Pollock

YaYo, Pook and Sinica were on A-Yard, walking the track conversating about how YaYo had just got the life sentence off his back and now only had four years left to serve on his ten-year sentence. His homies were happy that their comrade had another chance at life. YaYo had been back at Pollock for a week now and was trying to adjust to being at the prison. He had only been gone for about thirty days. In that short period of time, a lot of things had happened. Pook had informed YaYo that the Crips and Bloods had a riot all because one of the Crips named, Loco couldn't handle his liquor. Because of that a few good men had got stabbed and was now in the SHU awaiting transfer.

YaYo also found out that a guy he knew named, Face from Atlanta had stabbed one of his homies over some he said she said shit. Pollock was a breeding ground for violence. YaYo didn't have time for it and couldn't afford to put his out-date in jeopardy. The thought of going home to his family was all the morale he needed to motivate him to take the right steps in changing his life for the better.

"So, did you see some bad bitches out there?" Sinica asked interested in what was going on in the free world. Being gone over twenty years, the only thing the prison allowed him to see outside of the Penitentiary was the sky.

"Yeah, my nigga, them bitches definitely out there looking good."

"What's going on out there in the city? I know you was out visiting like a muthafucka," Pook said adjusting his shank in the front of his pants.

"It ain't the same shit that was going on when we was out there, my nigga. Niggas out there getting they head busted. The murda rate all the way up and niggas ain't got no integrity or dignity no more."

"Why you say that?"

"The game all fucked up, Pook. Shit used to be about loyalty and principals and shit. Now that shit don't mean nothing. A nigga can be a cold-blooded rat, as long as he got the bag niggas still gon' fuck with him. You can grow up with a nigga from the sandbox, been through trials and tribulations with the nigga and all. You get your bands up and he don't feel he equal to you. Nigga get on some envy shit and blow your brains out. Shit crazy out there," YaYo said.

He knew the streets were not the same, loyalty didn't exist anymore and the man with the money was the boss. Didn't matter if he was a snitch, a faggot or straight up just a soft ass nigga, who didn't deserve the money he had in his clutch. Real niggas in the game was now the minority and the suckas were the majority.

"So, what you gonna do when you get out, YaYo?" Sinica asked.

"I'm gon' get out there and do what I have to do to stay out of prison. I'ma get a job first and take shit one day at a time." YaYo had four years to come up with a plan to be successful.

Four years wasn't a lot of time so every minute and every hour had to be used in planning for his release and his future. The three convicts continue to walk the track and enjoy their time together all was positive mind-frames until the move was called. YaYo had a lot to do as he made his route toward the library to get up with Mr. B, his friend, and his mentor.

As he walked into the prison library YaYo noticed, Mr. B, sitting at the computer typing away. His focus was on what he was doing when YaYo walked up.

"What's up, Mr. B, tell me something good!" YaYo greeted.

Mr. B looked up at YaYo and smiled. "Hey, look what the wind just blew in!" Mr. B extended his hand and shook YaYo's hand. "So, how you feel youngsta? Feel like you got the weight of the world off your back, don't it?"

"Mr. B, I can't even lie, it doesn't even seem real," YaYo replied and took a seat next to Mr. B

"Well, I'ma tell you this, Yaton. You better start acting like it's real because it definitely is. Four years is not a long time before you know it they will be calling you to R&D to pack out and push you on your way back to Chicago. So, you have to have your shit together, young brother."

"Yeah, I know Mr. B, I'ma start by getting my G.E.D. I already signed up for school. So, I'm going to work towards that."

"I'm glad to hear that, Yaton. Education is the key to success, my brother. The white folks try to keep us blinded. You knew how, Yaton?"

"How, Mr. B?"

"They put the valuable information that we need to survive in the book! They know young black men and women don't read a lot. We would rather watch Love and Hip-Hop and all the rest of these fake reality shows. Consuming our minds with gangsta rap that promotes guns, drugs, sex, and violence. Now I judge nobody or what they read, watch or listen to but how can you learn from that kind of material?"

"You make sense, Mr. B."

"Yaton, I wish you woulda gotten free when you went to court. That was our plan, but at the same time, Yaton, I don't feel that you are ready. Ready to do what we discussed. To hold up your side of the bargain. You didn't forget about our agreement already did you?" Mr. B asked with a smirk.

"Not at all, Mr. B. Matter of fact, Mr. B I wanted to holla at you about something."

"What's that?"

"Remember you invited me to have the Nation of Islam speech at the Chapel?"

"I remember."

"Well, if it's not too much to ask I would like to go with you on Friday."

Mr. B smiled he had waited a long time for YaYo to speak these exact words. He had invited YaYo once or twice before and each time YaYo refused. So, he figured when YaYo felt he was ready he would come around. He didn't want to force Islam upon him. Now Mr. B saw his vision in hindsight, if YaYo accepted Allah as his one and only God, then Mr. B's plan and goals would flourish.

"Yaton, it is definitely alright with me. I'm proud of you Yaton."

"Why is that, Mr. B?" YaYo asked.

"For choosing life over death. Youngster, it's all about growth and development. To live is to live as to stand still is to die."

"Well, Mr. B I'm definitely not trying to die," YaYo replied.

"Well, meet at the chapel tomorrow on the 12:30 and let's see if we can get you started on your path to righteousness."

It was 12:30 in the afternoon as the 100-degree weather scorched the prison yard. The 12:30 move had just been called and YaYo and Mr. B were on their way to the chapel for religious service. YaYo didn't know what to expect from the Nation of Islam service but was interested. Mr.B had spoken so passionately about the Nation of Islam and YaYo couldn't wait to find out what had Mr. B so peaceful. As they walked into the chapel, YaYo saw a crowd of black men posted all over the chapel until everybody took a seat in the chair that was facing the podium. A dark-skinned, bald brother walked up and adjusted the microphone before he spoke, "As-Salaam-Alaikum."

"Wa-Alaikum Salaam," the crowd said in return.

"Can we all rise and face the East, arms in front of us with our palms up?" The men said a prayer that YaYo had never heard and then they sat back down.

"Good Evening, my brothers!" the man said, his Muslim name was Hasan but his name on the compound was Black.

Black was from the Southside of Chicago but was indicted in Madison Wisconsin where he controlled the lucrative drug trade until a close friend turned government informant and gave them information that would seal Black's faith with a life-sentence. Being down for seventeen years, Black began to study Islam and was introduced to the Nation and accepted the Honorable Elijah Muhammad as the prophet of Allah. Black took to the microphone.

"My brothers today we are going to talk about Prophets and Messengers. My brothers, we must get into the condition and position of no longer being deprived of the natural needs of the human being, such as freedom, justice, equality. The love of self, the love of their own kind. The unity of self, the power of self and that people are unable to find their own way out of that condition, out of the mercy of Allah. He always raises from the midst of that into particular knowledge that they need in order to be successful."

****

"Y'all think KI, ready?" Goon asked from the back seat of the tinted Chrysler Twin and Country Minivan.

They were parked directly on the side of, Pete's Firearms and Sporting Goods. Lil' Marcus sat beside him putting the 30-round clip into his .40. Omega sat behind the steering wheel pulling his black hoodie over his bald tattooed head, while Ace sat in the passenger seat with the AK-47 laying across his lap looking at his iPhone.

He said, "Two more minutes."

"Ki, gon be mad as shit!" Goon said laughing from the backseat.

The homicide crew had driven the 12-hour drive to Summerville to take the gun store down and everybody was starting to get antsy.

"One more minute."

The crew began to slide the masks over their faces to conceal their identities. After everybody was locked and loaded ready to get active. Ace grabbed his cell phone and sent a text.

After sending the text he said to his homies, "Let's get it, my niggas."

Ki had just felt Pete's Pecker began to stiffen when her phone vibrated in the pocket of her tight jeans. Pete was about to shoot his load when Ki pushed him forcefully away from her. Sprung to her feet and went in her Doone and Burk handbag to retrieve the chrome .357 snub nose and pointed it at Pete.

"Ole, what's gotten into you?" Pete asked shocked at the change of events.

Without warning, she stepped up and slapped him with the steel to get his mind right. The weapon caused his skin on his bald head to spit like Moses split the red sea. Blood gushed from the flesh wound that had been inflicted. Ki grabbed him forcefully by the collar of his t-shirt that was now stained with blood, forcing him to the front of the store. Where four gunmen awaited him.

"Tie his bitch ass up!" Ki commended and kicked him in his ass as hard as she could making him fall flat on his face in front of Omega who pulled the plastic ties from his hoodie and began to secure the door. Ace posted up at the entrance of the gun store with the AK-47. While Ki, Omega, Goon and Lil' Marcus raced to the back of the store.

"In here y'all!" Ki said and led them into the room where all the boxes were located.

Omega opened up a box that had **FNH** in big bold letters on it, in it read FNH, S. 62 caliber handguns. The rounds for the FNH were armor-piercing. Omega grabbed the box and rushed out to the van to put the box in it. Ki found a box loaded with Glock '40s. The crew made numerous trips from the store to the van filling it with artillery. Lil' Marcus looked on the wall and saw the historic machine gun and his eyes got big as a golf ball staring at the Thompson Machine Gun also known as the Tommy-Gun. He had to have it, he stood on top of a case and grabbed the Tommy off the wall.

Ace looked at his watch. "Time—let's bounce up outta here."

"What about this motherfucker?" Omega asked.

Before anybody could answer Ki walked up to Pete, pointed to the large revolver at him at point-blank range and pulled the trigger. *Boom!* She blew his brains out, blood poured from the large hole in his head covering the floor beneath him with the sticky fluid that smelled of copper. The loud gunshot caused their ears to ring and the rest of the crew was definitely shocked at her boldness. Lil' Marcus looked down at the dead corpse that was sprawled across the floor, witnessing the murder happen only a few feet away from him and the fresh aroma of death made him throw up.

"You good, my nigga?" Ace's rifle was now pointed at Lil' Marcus.

Omega and Ace were destined hitters, Goon was a natural head bussa and Ki was sick, the brains leaking out of Pete's melon confirmed it. Nobody knew if Lil' Marcus was capable of murder or holding water for that matter

"Yeah, I'm good," Lil' Marcus replied wiping the vomit from the corner of his mouth

"You sure?" Ki said walking up to Lil' Marcus with the .357 still hot.

"Yeah, I'm straight."

Pointing the snub nose at the dead body Ki said, "Bust your gun then, nigga!"

Lil' Marcus raised the .40 toward Pete's soulless body. He had never killed anybody or shot somebody in his life. Even though he knew Pete was already dead he was still a little nervous but knew he was put on the spot and if he didn't do as instructed he would be lying next to Pete.

Boc! Boc! Boc! The .40 jerked in his hand while the shell casings littered the floor. Ki smiled before she made a dash towards the door. Omega was about to follow suit until he looked around and made face to face contact with the store's security camera

"Hold up!" Omega ran to the back of the store, three minutes later he came back with two discs, from the security camera. Ace, Goon, and Lil' Marcus ran out of Pete's Firearm and Sporting Goods, with plenty of guns, amenities and a dead body. On their way back to the city of Chi, the homicide crew was now equipped to take the city under siege, in the midst of their crimes, a lot of families were about to mourn for their deceased loved ones.

S. Allen

CHAPTER 31

"I'll tell you one damn thing if they let Trump get reelected he gon' do some stupid ass shit to start a world war. Watch what I tell you. Shit, I can do a better job being the president then that clown," Karen said to Chanel.

Karen was at her beauty salon taking care of one of her regulars. She didn't really get into politics but was not a fan of Donald Trump at all.

"Girl that cracker right there definitely got some issues. All he cares about is building the damn wall, they need to put his ass in Mexico, then build the wall!" Chanel replied and they both busted out laughing.

Karen felt comfort at her beauty salon and not to mention her steady clientele on a daily basis had the money coming in good. This provided her a good life even though she was single. She still stood on her business, she was grateful that her son, Yaton had invested some of his money into the beauty salon. Because if not she didn't know where she would be at this point in her life. Being single was hard and she had a lot to deal with, even doing well financially she still had to face single-handedly what we all have in life at times, problems.

Her oldest son was doing time in a federal penitentiary, one of her sons could barely walk due to gun violence and her other son had now devoted his life to the streets, but with all the drama Karen still remained in control and in a positive mind-frame. She prayed to God to wash all her problems away.

Karen had just finished doing Chanel's hair when a Cherry Red Maserati Levante pulled up in front of the shop.

"Girl look at that pretty ass car!" An excited Chanel said pointing to the shiny foreign vehicle.

A tall, dark-skinned gentleman with black, wavy hair stepped out of the car, his pin-striped suit looked expensive while the watch on his left wrist shined the moment the sun rays hit it.

Karen squinted her eyes trying to get a better look at the very familiar face as the man-made his way toward the entrance of the shop. As he got closer to the door, Karen couldn't believe who it was, she hadn't seen him in almost four years and hadn't spoken to him in almost two. It was like he had disappeared off the face of the earth, now entering her place of business was her estranged husband, Darrell. He walked into the beauty salon Darrell took his shades off to get a better look at his beautiful wife who he hadn't seen in years. Karen couldn't keep her emotions in check as she briskly walked up on him and slapped the shit out of him. The contact from her palm connecting to his face caused his jaw to sting. He knew he had that coming.

"How dare you walk into my place of business? Your son was shot in the streets and has been confined to a wheelchair. Your mother knew what was going on because she was at the hospital at his bedside. And you just now show your face?" Tears began to swell in Karen's brown eyes.

"Baby, you walked out on me."

"What the fuck that got to do with, Davon and Quavon?"

Darrell tried to choose his words carefully before he spoke. "Karen—I couldn't see my son laid up in the hospital like that. It would have crushed me," Darrell said in his defense.

"Well, I think it crushed Davon to not have his father by his side when he needed him most."

"You took my kids and walked out of my life for no reason."

"*No reason*? You treated Yaton like he was a piece of shit, my blood son. How could I be with somebody who doesn't even love my chile? You terrorized him he was so innocent Darrell! You made him move to Chicago and forced him to adapt to street life. I shoulda never let you do that. It's your fault he is in Federal Prison. It's your fault, Davon cannot walk. And it is your fault, Quavon has turned into the demon he is!" Karen cried as her blood boiled.

While her tears stained her cheeks. The words Karen spoke made Darrell feel guilty about his actions. When he first met, Karen was seventeen-years-old with one child. He had just moved from Miami Florida to start his life over after coming home for doing a two-year federal sentence which he served in Marica Illinois for a white-collar crime. While in prison Darrell changed his life for the better. Being the go-getter that he was his vision to be a real estate agent began to flourish once he was released from prison. Starting Darrell's real estate in Chicago he climbed to his success wasn't easy as he thought. But his hard work and strongly driven ambition would pave the way to his future.

After meeting Karen on a cruise he instantly fell in love with the 5'5, mocha-colored beauty queen. Approaching her as the gentlemen he was the two of them hit it off well. To say he spoke and treated her as the queen she was would be an understatement. Karen was now exposed to the finer things in life, vacations to California, Paris, designer clothes and steak dinners were just a few of the perks of dating the young smart goal driven man she was with. Darrell had also learned to love Karen's only child, Yaton. He treated him as if he was his own even calling him his son at three-years-old.

Yaton looked to Darrell as his father because Darrell was the only figure in his life at the time. His biological father died in a horrible car accident. Darrell had the woman of his dreams and asked for her hand in marriage which resulted in her giving birth to two healthy baby boys, Quavon and Davon. Darrell was the happiest man in the world as he held his sons in his arms. He had never felt so much joy or pride in his life and it was at that moment his love for Yaton began to fade away. The fatherly love he once held for Yaton was now replaced with anger, resentment and child abuse.

Karen was confused at why Darrell had suddenly started treating Yaton different. Things begin to get worse when Darrell's Real Estate company began to fall apart and the mortgage for the Condo the family lived in began to fall behind. Darrell's frustration of his financial situation caused him to take it out on his wife and at that point in time, the physical abuse started as well as the drug use. Darrell would jump in his Benz and drive to Humbolt Park an area on the Westside of the city governed by the Latin Kings, a Hispanic gang to purchase crack-cocaine.

Darrell would smoke the addictive drug to combat the trials and tribulations he was facing in his life. Things only got worse as his mood swings were more and more, thus making the physical abuse toward his wife and step-son more routine. The night Darrell beat,

Yaton unconscious was the last time he had laid hands on Yaton. Karen couldn't take it anymore and sent Yaton to live with his grandmother. She had enough of Darrell and his physical abuse and later in life left him altogether. That was four years ago and now here it was Darrell was standing before her like he hadn't caused the mental and physical pain upon her.

"Karen, listen, I'm sorry for how I treated Yaton and you. I have had a lot of time to reflect on the decisions that I made. I was wrong, point blank period. If I could turn back the hands of time I would, but I can't. It hurts me to know that I am the cause of how Yaton's life turned out. I was young and I knew nothing about being a father. I owe you an apology. I came here to see, Davon. I was also hoping to get my wife back." Karen looked at Darrell like he had just lost his mind. Apart of her still loved him but a part of her hated his guts. Darrell continued, "I was thinking that both of us could go see Davon. It's a lot I want to say to him. I also need to find that hard-headed son of mines. He doesn't have to hustle in the streets anymore or do whatever he is out there doing. I'm in a position to help him."

"Is that right?"

"Yes, I also want to know where Yaton is serving his time. I want to go and see him. I have a lot of explaining to do to him and it has been well overdue."

Karen's defensive attitude was brought down a notch at Darrell's last comment. If Darrell wanted to get in contact with Yaton then she knew Darrell had grown mentally but she also knew words held less value. It was all about the action.

"How about I pick you up after work? We can go and see Davon and all go out for dinner. Then take it from there."

Karen looked into Darrell's eyes trying to read them for any sign of deceit or betrayal but all she saw was guilt and sincerity in them. At that moment she wanted to embrace her husband and cry into his chest for all the pain she had been through. Deep inside she missed him but at the same time, he had broken her heart and betrayed her trust. However, she wouldn't be selfish, Davon needed his father and so did Quavon. For that reason alone, she decided to let Darrell back in her life.

"I get off at six, you can meet me at Mt. Sini Hospital."

Darrell smiled a warm smile. "Thank you, Karen, for giving me a chance," he said.

He hugged her and made his way toward the door leaving the smell of his *Issey Miyake* after his departure. Karen watched as he left and pulled out in his expensive vehicle. It felt like a little weight had been lifted off her shoulders, she just hoped and prayed she had just made the right decision.

S. Allen

CHAPTER 32
Quavon

I know y'all saying the money changed me. I'ma tell y'all what changed me, catching my first body. The day I blew Butterball's brain out changed my life. It stained my soul and at that point, there was no turning back. I grew up following in my brother's steps. I was infatuated with him and his street reputation. The streets respected him and his team and I wanted in. I didn't get to the top by myself. The jewels my brother gave me before he went to the FEDs guided me through the blood, sweat, and tears that we all call the game. The most important piece of game my brother gave me was to think before I move. Life was chess not checkers, loyalty and trust bonded men.

T.B.'s disloyalty and blatant disrespect went against G.B.C rules so his violation was a death sentence. He was playing games with a grown man. I killed his grandmother because I had to show the streets, I was cold. The only way to survive in Chi-Raq was to be cold, so now I'ma beast. Top Cat was a piece of cake. He underestimated me, he was blinded by the money and drugs. His thirst for money caused his demise, I had a thirst for power. Nothing means nothing without the other. After my twin got shot my inner savage was unleashed. No longer am I, schoolboy, Quavon, my team is ruthless and murderous, letting nobody step on our toes or eat off our plate. The sky is our limit and for y'all still reading, this is only the beginning.

To Be Continued...
Yayo 3
Coming Soon

Submission Guideline

Submit the first three chapters of your completed manuscript to ldpsubmissions@gmail.com, subject line: Your book's title. The manuscript must be in a .doc file and sent as an attachment. Document should be in Times New Roman, double spaced and in size 12 font. Also, provide your synopsis and full contact information. If sending multiple submissions, they must each be in a separate email.

Have a story but no way to send it electronically? You can still submit to LDP/Ca$h Presents. Send in the first three chapters, written or typed, of your completed manuscript to:

LDP: Submissions Dept
Po Box 870494
Mesquite, Tx 75187

DO NOT send original manuscript. Must be a duplicate.

Provide your synopsis and a cover letter containing your full contact information.

Thanks for considering LDP and Ca$h Presents.

YAYO

Coming Soon from Lock Down Publications/Ca$h Presents

BOW DOWN TO MY GANGSTA

By **Ca$h**

TORN BETWEEN TWO

By **Coffee**

THE STREETS STAINED MY SOUL **II**

By **Marcellus Allen**

BLOOD OF A BOSS **VI**

SHADOWS OF THE GAME II

By **Askari**

LOYAL TO THE GAME **IV**

By **T.J. & Jelissa**

A DOPEBOY'S PRAYER **II**

By **Eddie "Wolf" Lee**

IF LOVING YOU IS WRONG… **III**

By **Jelissa**

TRUE SAVAGE **VII**

MIDNIGHT CARTEL

DOPE BOY MAGIC II

By **Chris Green**

BLAST FOR ME **III**

DUFFLE BAG CARTEL **IV**

HEARTLESS GOON **IV**

A SAVAGE DOPEBOY II

DRUG LORDS III

By **Ghost**

A HUSTLER'S DECEIT III

KILL ZONE **II**

BAE BELONGS TO ME III

S. Allen

SOUL OF A MONSTER III
By **Aryanna**
THE COST OF LOYALTY **III**
By **Kweli**
THE SAVAGE LIFE III
CHAINED TO THE STREETS II
By **J-Blunt**
KING OF NEW YORK V
COKE KINGS IV
BORN HEARTLESS IV
By **T.J. Edwards**
GORILLAZ IN THE BAY V
De'Kari
THE STREETS ARE CALLING II
Duquie Wilson
KINGPIN KILLAZ IV
STREET KINGS III
PAID IN BLOOD III
CARTEL KILLAZ IV
Hood Rich
SINS OF A HUSTLA II
ASAD
TRIGGADALE III
Elijah R. Freeman
KINGZ OF THE GAME V
Playa Ray
SLAUGHTER GANG IV
RUTHLESS HEART II
By Willie Slaughter
THE HEART OF A SAVAGE II

YAYO

By Jibril Williams

FUK SHYT II

By Blakk Diamond

THE DOPEMAN'S BODYGAURD II

By Tranay Adams

TRAP GOD II

By Troublesome

YAYO III

A SHOOTER'S AMBITION II

By S. Allen

GHOST MOB

Stilloan Robinson

KINGPIN DREAMS II

By Paper Boi Rari

CREAM

By Yolanda Moore

SON OF A DOPE FIEND II

By Renta

FOREVER GANGSTA II

By Adrian Dulan

LOYALTY AIN'T PROMISED

By Keith Williams

THE PRICE YOU PAY FOR LOVE II

By Destiny Skai

THE LIFE OF A HOOD STAR

By Rashia Wilson

TOE TAGZ II

By Ah'Million

CONFESSIONS OF A GANGSTA II

By Nicholas Lock

Available Now

RESTRAINING ORDER **I & II**
By **CA$H & Coffee**
LOVE KNOWS NO BOUNDARIES **I II & III**
By **Coffee**
RAISED AS A GOON I, II, III & IV
BRED BY THE SLUMS I, II, III
BLAST FOR ME I & II
ROTTEN TO THE CORE I II III
A BRONX TALE I, II, III
DUFFEL BAG CARTEL I II III
HEARTLESS GOON
A SAVAGE DOPEBOY
HEARTLESS GOON I II III
DRUG LORDS I II
By **Ghost**
LAY IT DOWN **I & II**
LAST OF A DYING BREED
BLOOD STAINS OF A SHOTTA I & II III
By **Jamaica**
LOYAL TO THE GAME
LOYAL TO THE GAME II
LOYAL TO THE GAME III
LIFE OF SIN I, II III
By **TJ & Jelissa**
BLOODY COMMAS I & II
SKI MASK CARTEL I II & III
KING OF NEW YORK I II,III IV

YAYO

RISE TO POWER I II III

COKE KINGS I II III

BORN HEARTLESS I II III

By **T.J. Edwards**

IF LOVING HIM IS WRONG…I & II

LOVE ME EVEN WHEN IT HURTS I II III

By **Jelissa**

WHEN THE STREETS CLAP BACK I & II III

By **Jibril Williams**

A DISTINGUISHED THUG STOLE MY HEART I II & III

LOVE SHOULDN'T HURT I II III IV

RENEGADE BOYS I II III IV

By **Meesha**

A GANGSTER'S CODE I &, II III

A GANGSTER'S SYN I II III

THE SAVAGE LIFE I II

CHAINED TO THE STREETS

By **J-Blunt**

PUSH IT TO THE LIMIT

By **Bre' Hayes**

BLOOD OF A BOSS **I, II, III, IV, V**

SHADOWS OF THE GAME

By **Askari**

THE STREETS BLEED MURDER **I, II & III**

THE HEART OF A GANGSTA I II& III

By **Jerry Jackson**

CUM FOR ME

CUM FOR ME 2

CUM FOR ME 3

CUM FOR ME 4

CUM FOR ME 5

An **LDP Erotica Collaboration**

BRIDE OF A HUSTLA **I II & II**

THE FETTI GIRLS **I, II& III**

CORRUPTED BY A GANGSTA I, II III, IV

BLINDED BY HIS LOVE

THE PRICE YOU PAY FOR LOVE

By **Destiny Skai**

WHEN A GOOD GIRL GOES BAD

By **Adrienne**

THE COST OF LOYALTY I II

By Kweli

A GANGSTER'S REVENGE **I II III & IV**

THE BOSS MAN'S DAUGHTERS

THE BOSS MAN'S DAUGHTERS II

THE BOSSMAN'S DAUGHTERS III

THE BOSSMAN'S DAUGHTERS IV

THE BOSS MAN'S DAUGHTERS **V**

A SAVAGE LOVE **I & II**

BAE BELONGS TO ME I II

A HUSTLER'S DECEIT I, II, III

WHAT BAD BITCHES DO I, II, III

SOUL OF A MONSTER I II

KILL ZONE

By **Aryanna**

A KINGPIN'S AMBITON

A KINGPIN'S AMBITION **II**

I MURDER FOR THE DOUGH

By **Ambitious**

TRUE SAVAGE

YAYO

TRUE SAVAGE II

TRUE SAVAGE **III**

TRUE SAVAGE **IV**

TRUE SAVAGE **V**

TRUE SAVAGE **VI**

DOPE BOY MAGIC

MIDNIGHT CARTEL

By **Chris Green**

A DOPEBOY'S PRAYER

By **Eddie "Wolf" Lee**

THE KING CARTEL **I, II & III**

By **Frank Gresham**

THESE NIGGAS AIN'T LOYAL **I, II & III**

By **Nikki Tee**

GANGSTA SHYT **I II &III**

By **CATO**

THE ULTIMATE BETRAYAL

By **Phoenix**

BOSS'N UP **I , II & III**

By **Royal Nicole**

I LOVE YOU TO DEATH

By Destiny J

I RIDE FOR MY HITTA

I STILL RIDE FOR MY HITTA

By **Misty Holt**

LOVE & CHASIN' PAPER

By **Qay Crockett**

TO DIE IN VAIN

SINS OF A HUSTLA

By **ASAD**

S. Allen

BROOKLYN HUSTLAZ

By **Boogsy Morina**

BROOKLYN ON LOCK I & II

By **Sonovia**

GANGSTA CITY

By **Teddy Duke**

A DRUG KING AND HIS DIAMOND I & II III

A DOPEMAN'S RICHES

HER MAN, MINE'S TOO I, II

CASH MONEY HO'S

By Nicole Goosby

TRAPHOUSE KING **I II & III**

KINGPIN KILLAZ I II III

STREET KINGS I II

PAID IN BLOOD **I II**

CARTEL KILLAZ I II III

By **Hood Rich**

LIPSTICK KILLAH **I, II, III**

CRIME OF PASSION I II & III

By **Mimi**

STEADY MOBBN' **I, II, III**

THE STREETS STAINED MY SOUL

By **Marcellus Allen**

WHO SHOT YA **I, II, III**

SON OF A DOPE FIEND

Renta

GORILLAZ IN THE BAY **I II III IV**

DE'KARI

TRIGGADALE I II

Elijah R. Freeman

216

YAYO

GOD BLESS THE TRAPPERS I, II, III
THESE SCANDALOUS STREETS I, II, III
FEAR MY GANGSTA I, II, III
THESE STREETS DON'T LOVE NOBODY I, II
BURY ME A G I, II, III, IV, V
A GANGSTA'S EMPIRE I, II, III, IV
THE DOPEMAN'S BODYGAURD
Tranay Adams
THE STREETS ARE CALLING
Duquie Wilson
MARRIED TO A BOSS... I II III
By Destiny Skai & Chris Green
KINGZ OF THE GAME I II III IV
Playa Ray
SLAUGHTER GANG I II III
RUTHLESS HEART
By Willie Slaughter
THE HEART OF A SAVAGE
By Jibril Williams
FUK SHYT
By Blakk Diamond
DON'T F#CK WITH MY HEART I II
By Linnea
ADDICTED TO THE DRAMA I II III
By Jamila
YAYO I II
A SHOOTER'S AMBITION
By S. Allen
TRAP GOD
By Troublesome

217

FOREVER GANGSTA
By Adrian Dulan
TOE TAGZ
By Ah'Million
KINGPIN DREAMS
By Paper Boi Rari
CONFESSIONS OF A GANGSTA
By Nicholas Lock

BOOKS BY LDP'S CEO, CA$H

TRUST IN NO MAN
TRUST IN NO MAN 2
TRUST IN NO MAN 3
BONDED BY BLOOD
SHORTY GOT A THUG
THUGS CRY
THUGS CRY 2
THUGS CRY 3
TRUST NO BITCH
TRUST NO BITCH 2
TRUST NO BITCH 3
TIL MY CASKET DROPS
RESTRAINING ORDER
RESTRAINING ORDER 2
IN LOVE WITH A CONVICT

Coming Soon
BONDED BY BLOOD 2
BOW DOWN TO MY GANGSTA

S. Allen